PIG DOG CREEK

KATHLEEN STOCKMIER

Kathy,
I hope you enjoy
"Pig Dog Creek."
Best Wishes,
Kathleen Stockmier
9/24/16

Copyright © 2016 Kathleen Louise Stockmier

This book is a work of fiction. Names, characters, businesses, places, events and incidents are either the products of the author's imagination or used in a fictitious manner. Any resemblance to actual persons, living or dead, or actual events is purely coincidental.

All rights reserved. No part of this book may be reproduced or transmitted in any form whatsoever.

ISBN-13: 978-0-9977939-0-1

ISBN-10: 0997793902

To Shine & Whitey

CONTENTS

Chapter 1: The Creek 6

Chapter 2: The Book 11

Chapter 3: The Cloud 15

Chapter 4: The Deal 19

Chapter 5: The Setting 26

Chapter 6: The Daisies 29

Chapter 7: The Emergency 33

Chapter 8: The Swine 41

Chapter 9: The Hospital 46

Chapter 10: The Encounter 53

Chapter 11: The Sucker 60

Chapter 12: The Pencil 62

Chapter 13: Rock of Ages 66

Chapter 14: The Contract 71

Chapter 15: The Stand 75

Chapter 16: The Pie 78

Chapter 17: The Fork 81

Chapter 18: The Goodbye 86

Chapter 19: The News 91

Chapter 20: Freedom 97

Chapter 21: Verneice 105

Chapter 22: The Wait 109

Chapter 23: The Grocery Store 113

Chapter 24: The Deed 119

Chapter 25: The Lighter 124

Chapter 26: The Key 129

Chapter 27: The Rain 137

Chapter 28: The Body 146

Chapter 29: The Dream 155

Chapter 30: The Knot 164

Chapter 31: The Surprise 170

AKNOWLEDGMENTS

This fictitious book and all its colorful characters have been a part of my life for about 15 years, and I am so excited to have it in print to share with others.

On this journey from rough draft to print, there have been many willing readers, editors, artists and supporters who have helped and encouraged me. My husband, Barry, and daughter, Lisa, have been my constant cheerleaders. Others in the rooting section include English professors Dr. Nancy Castilla and Richard Abshire.

My journalism students gave me a lot of support and encouragement over the years, too. And my neighbor, mentor and friend, Ann Pearle, created the beautiful art for the cover.

There are so many more people to thank, but I'm afraid I'll leave someone out, so here's to everyone who helped me finally get this manuscript to print!

FOREWORD

Creeks are like people. They flow through life accumulating possessions that are either kept or discarded along their journey.

They swell in times of good weather and dry up in drought, flowing from one place to another, collecting valuables or discarded trophies along the way, and either dumping them into tributaries or absorbing them into their viscera.

To many, a creek appears to be nothing but a nuisance, like a scavenger who's too lazy to work and feeds off the generosity of others. But many see its charm and big-hearted nature. While its topside might appear to be rough, moody or ruthless, its personality is often calming.

It's the creek's smooth underbelly – its most vulnerable area – where secrets abide.

On this underside, skeletons of deeds gone wrong haunt its passage. Unforgiving sins, harrowing memories, and resentment reach up to its free-spirited topside every now and then to jolt its equilibrium.

But nothing can stop the creeks from their voyages.

****

No one knows exactly how Pig Dog Creek got its name. As long as folks in Cook, Tennessee, can remember, Pig Dog has always been called Pig Dog.

There are those who swear on the graves of their kinfolk that a litter of pups with a dead mother wound up suckling a pig to stay alive, and how those pups grew up along the creek to be the meanest dogs in town, terrorizing people and their livestock.

Generations of Cook's residents have passed down the story of that "litter of mean critters" and their rampage on Cook. But over the years, that tale has slowly been replaced with one about a single dog named Buster, the runt of that mean litter, who preferred solitude rather than a life of crime like his siblings; a dog who stayed behind and lived along the banks of the creek scavenging for food, eating anything that the townsfolk would throw his way or he could catch in the wild on his own.

He never barked or growled or bothered anyone or anything. You wouldn't have even known he existed unless you were hunting squirrel and tripped over his sleeping body.

Buster sightings were rare, but word around Cook – whether genuine or fabricated – was that the dog was a crossbreed of pig and dog, and had the ugliest face they'd ever seen on an animal.

The stories vary with each yarn spinner, but almost all of them agree that the dog's snout resembled that of a pig, and his tail was coiled, too.

###

INTRODUCTION

May 1962

    Cook, Tennessee, is like most small farming communities in the northwestern portion of The Volunteer State. Located about ten miles east of the Mississippi River, Cook has residents that are laid-back and friendly, honest and hard-working, and generally know everything that goes on in their neighbors' lives.

    There's a cluster of homes in Cook nestled together at the bottom of a small mountain where most of the residents live. The houses are small, except for those whose families own hundreds of acres of farmland or run businesses in nearby Herndon. They are sturdy and modest, some in better shape than others, and each backyard is in perfect earshot of their neighbor's open kitchen window. Most of the yards are fenceless, but chicken wire or chain link barriers occasionally dot the land to keep children or farm animals in, and the "critters of the creek" out.

    Pig Dog Creek weaves behind the homes and is only visible from the main road by the line of trees that follow its course. Every now and then there's a footpath parting those trees, and a tire swing is not an uncommon sight to see hanging from one of the huge oaks.

    There are more homes up in the hills, but the higher you travel on the winding dirt road, the more rundown they get. Hidden by trees and overgrown shrubs, the dwellings are not inviting. Many of the families do not have electricity or indoor plumbing. Animals run loose on the property, and junk vehicles crowd the landscape. "Keep Out" signs are abundant along the route.

    A creek is like the thread that sews the community together in Tennessee's rural towns. A town without a creek has no order, the locals say. Without it, there is nothing that connects the people to the land. It digs and weaves its way through a town's real estate creating a fortress, so to speak, whether real or imaginary. It's surprising, though, how these revered passages are given such hideous names, but when you consider the strange monikers given to some of its residents, these names can only be considered as terms of endearment.

The roads surrounding the homes are dirt, creating lots of dust that blows through the window screens in dry and windy weather, to mud that's stuck to shoes and trampled inside when it's wet. There's a general store with a U.S. Post Office inside, a gas station, cotton gin, a jail with one temporary holding cell, a Baptist Church, and a schoolhouse for grades one through eight. The teenagers ride a bus to Herndon High School on the tarred road that connects the farming community to the world.

Education isn't a high priority. Survival is. If it means quitting school to work the cotton fields so mouths can be fed, then so be it. That could account for the simple street names printed by hand on t-shaped posts. But it doesn't matter if you live on Hog Lane or Cow Road when it comes to receiving mail. None of the houses have numbers, because all of the mail is delivered to the post office located inside the general store and sorted into slots tagged with each resident's surname. Besides the addressee's name, all that's required on the outside of an envelope is "Cook, Tennessee."

Farming, hunting and fishing skills are passed from one son to another like rites of passage. Daughters learn to cook at an early age from their mothers and grandmothers, using recipes that have been passed down for generations, recipes that almost always require ingredients furnished by the land. Squirrel, rabbit, fish, collard greens, butter beans, pecan pie, potatoes, baking powder biscuits and homemade ice cream are just a few of the common dishes produced in Cook's kitchens.

The gathering spot is the porch of the general store where the men of Cook play dominoes and discuss local and national issues, issues about those "damn commies in Russia," the A-bomb, and President Kennedy wasting taxpayers' money to put a man in space when "people are starving here in America."

They talk about the threat of automated machinery that is going to "take over the world and do the work of hundreds of people," and that concerns them a little, but only one thing really has an effect on their livelihood as farmers – the weather. Rain is a good thing in Cook. On those days, the store's porch is crowded and the farmers are happier because they are more optimistic about harvesting profitable crops.

The topic of racial tension always makes its way into a daily discussion. The influx of Negroes moving from the south to the north is okay by them, but a hand-painted billboard on the outskirts of a town north of Cook that reads "If yer black, tern back" is debated as either senseless or necessary. "Just whut is this world a'comin' to?" is said more than ten times during one domino game, followed by everyone's heads shaking back and forth.

The women of Cook are left out of discussions of such worldly issues and are subservient to their husbands and families. It is the only way of life that they know and are allowed to enter, and there is no retaliation. It is a job they do well, and they are perfectly content giving the problems of the world to their husbands to solve. Women who try to compete or challenge the men on decisions and the "order of things" are thought of as "selfish and big-headed," even "whore-like."

But no one in Cook has a quarrel with ownership of people or property. If it's legally yours, you can do anything you want with it. Proprietorship is king. Backs have been turned when questionable situations have come forth, situations like making moonshine, gambling or incest. Despite these sins, the morals of Cook's residents are high because Jesus is Lord, and He is Baptist.

And that's why a 12-year-old girl named Annie was traded to a family for three bags of unshelled pecans and held prisoner in her home in 1962 America – because it wasn't the sin of a town, but the sins of two families. And those family members would have to answer to that some day, either on earth or at the Pearly Gates.

1 / THE CREEK

Cook, Tennessee, 1962

A mysterious speck of light seeping through a small slit in the tattered window shade danced around Annie Barton's eyes and awakened her from a fitful slumber. She was confused by its soft glow in the dark house. It wasn't normal. Goose bumps popped up on her limbs. She ran her hands up and down each arm and then rubbed her closed eyes to clear them of sleep. When she opened them, the light was gone but she felt a powerful urgency to get out of the house and begin her morning ritual.

She slowly eased back the ragged quilt, lifted her naked body from the bed and tiptoed across the wooden floor toward the closet, pausing to grab her robe from a rusted hanger and to listen for any signs of life stirring within the house. The only sound she could hear was an annoying snort followed by a long snore that was coming from her husband's mouth. In thirty minutes he'd be awake, she thought, and the sun would be up to begin another day of hell.

She checked the robe's right pocket and smiled when she felt the bar of soap and washcloth. In the left pocket was a rolled-up hand towel. Moving cat-like across the bedroom floor and into the kitchen, she reached the back door safely without making a sound. After three years of sneaking out every morning to bathe in the creek behind the house, she knew every loose board in the floor, every squeak of the back doorknob and just how far to open the porch's screen door before it creaked loudly.

Once outside, Annie's bare feet descended lightly down the three wooden steps leading to the dirt path that ran alongside the garden. She picked up speed when she passed the last two rows of vegetables. By the time she reached the outhouse behind the barn, her pace was quick enough to hurdle the two-foot chicken wire fence with ease.

The cool May morning air slapped color to her cheeks as she fled across the open field to the trees lining the creek, and her goose bumps returned. While disrobing on the bank, she glanced back to the house. No lights.

Another successful escape.

Annie eased her body into the cold stream and heard the birds awakening in the trees, a sound she once thought odd to hear in the darkness when she first began the early morning ritual.

"I wish I wuz a bird," she said.

She tilted her head back into the moonlit water and felt a slight breeze across her face. The mighty oaks that lined the creek's bank swayed their branches like arms waving 'hello' to her. This place was her very own piece of heaven on earth, even if she had to steal it. Every second was precious and her timing had to be precise: Five minutes to float and enjoy the peacefulness; two minutes to wash her hair, one minute to scrub her privates and another minute for a quick overall lather before rinsing.

She floated on her back with her eyes closed, conjuring up an image of herself in a flowing white gown like she'd seen on a page of a movie star magazine that she found last spring blowing along the creek bank. The lady in the picture was blonde and skinny like her, and she was dancing with a man in a black suit. They were both smiling, happy to be alive, she thought, and Annie envisioned their life filled with nice words, pretty music, a white two-story house and a big fancy car.

Every morning she looked forward to the daydream, imagining herself as the woman being swept across the curtained room by the handsome man who stopped every now and then to whisper in her ear, "I love you, Annie Louise." And she imagined looking into his blue eyes and smiling back, almost fainting with excitement.

She was never going to be like the lady in the picture, she thought, and all the dreaming and all the praying in the world wasn't going to make it happen.

"Stupid, stupid, stupid!" she blurted harshly, slapping the water. "Nope, I'm always gonna live in dirt and be stupid in the head until Robert or his parents either beat me to death or my arms break off from totin' young-uns and hangin' warsh."

Or maybe she'd die like her mama who couldn't get her ninth baby out. "Poor Mama," she cried. "What an awful way to die."

She could never forgive her daddy. They hadn't spoken since the day they buried her mama five years ago, the day he brought Robert home from the funeral and said, "Annie Lou, this here's yore new husband. Y'all are gettin' hitched today."

It didn't matter that she was just 12 years old. But with her out of the house, there would be one less mouth to feed, and that meant only one thing to her daddy — more money for him to spend on whiskey from Uncle Deek's still.

She stood up and began to wash, wishing the soap would erase the face of her dead mama from her head forever. While rubbing the cloth across her puffed breasts flush with morning milk, she thought of her three children back in the house and hurried her bathing ritual. The fear of someone waking up and finding her gone set her mind reeling.

"My stars, I've done been gone too long," she said, as she dried her body with the small towel. "Now, don't get all in a fuss, Annie Lou," she voiced in a tone mimicking her mama. "Lots of time left b'fore the clock chimes. No light yonder through the trees. No rooster crowin'.

"Oh, but what if Robert gets up to pee? Or Becky starts squawkin'? What if..."

The dead silence halted Annie's worries: no bird sounds, no swaying trees, no splashing of the creek's water against the rock. *Just absolute quiet.* With the towel in one hand, she stood naked and motionless on the creek's bank, rolling her eyes to the left and then to the right of the creek until it rounded out of sight. Something wasn't right, but what was it? Squinting, she panned the bank across the water for any signs of movement. Her eyes widened when she noticed the water wasn't flowing around the bend. It was as still as the trees, as quiet as the birds.

She reached for her robe lying on the ground but she couldn't move a muscle to retrieve it. *Yer just scared*, she told herself. *Scared stiff, kinda like when Daddy Jack comes into yer bed when Robert ain't at home. Jest settle yerself down. There ain't no boogeyman gonna get you.*

She tried to unfurl her fingers from around the towel and drop it to the ground, but couldn't. Her eyes scrolled down her side and saw her hand, but it was like it belonged to someone else. Then she realized that if she could roll her eyes, she could probably move her mouth. *But why? To scream? For who? Robert? Daddy Jack or Mama D?* She'd rather die. Die right there on the creek bank, naked as a jaybird.

From behind, she felt a breeze at her heels that slowly drifted up to her buttocks and encircled her shoulders. Her golden locks dried instantly, blowing forward into her face like a blindfold. She thought about the woman in the Bible that Daddy Jack told her about, the one who turned to salt. He said it was going to happen to her if she told anyone about him climbing on top of her.

She closed her eyes tightly and braced herself for the pain of her body turning to salt grains and blowing into the creek. *But why was this happening? She hadn't told anyone about Daddy Jack!* She suspected Mama D already knew by the way she looked at her the mornings after he'd been to her room. *That house is too small for her not to hear him gruntin' like a pig in my bed.*

Then she thought of the handsome man in the black suit. *Good, Lord! God's punishing me for the dream!*

A bird cawed overhead and Annie opened her eyes and saw the trees across the creek swaying in the morning breeze. The water below in Pig Dog Creek continued its course east. She lifted the towel to her face to brush back the strands of hair that had blown into her mouth.

Her first impulse was to turn around toward the house. Still no lights. How long had she been standing there paralyzed? Five minutes? Ten minutes? *It has to be time to get back!*

She bent down, grabbed her robe from the ground and heard something fall out of it. Thinking it was probably a piece of wood or a rock, she put the robe on without taking a closer look. She stuffed the soap, washcloth and hand towel into her pockets and turned to walk toward the house when she realized the thump she heard could have been a turtle that had crawled inside her robe while she was in the creek. She knelt down and felt around on the ground with her hands and touched a clump of something.

Poor li'l guy, she thought, reaching for the turtle. *He could be stuck on his back with his fat li'l feet pedalin' like a bike to nowheres.*

Expecting to feel a cold, ridged belly, her hands instead felt something hard, like a square piece of wood. She picked it up and drew it closer to her eyes.

"It's a book!" she gasped. Annie wiped the dirt from its cover and stood up, wondering what to do with it. Instinctively, she glanced toward the house. Still no lights, but she could make out someone moving fast down the dirt path toward the barn.

"Good God, it's Robert!" she cried. "And he's a'comin' to get me!"

Annie's heart raced while watching the mammoth figure move swiftly in her direction. She knew all too well its temper and strength. Tears flowed from her eyes and she began groaning softly through her chattering teeth. And then, just like that, he was nowhere in sight. She stood frozen for several seconds before the slamming sound of the outhouse door put her at ease.

I gotta get back. Gotta sneak back while he's in there!

She darted toward the house and got halfway across the field before she realized her hand was still clutching the book.

What am I a'gonna do with this? I can't take this inside!

She looked frantically around for a place to hide the book and spied the well on the left side of the house. As she quietly stepped over the chicken wire fence, she heard Robert cough from inside the outhouse. Bravely, she walked briskly around the barn, past the vegetables and clothesline, leaving a puff of dirt at her heels along the path leading to the back steps. Behind her, she heard the outhouse door open and close again.

Forget the well, she decided, and stuffed the book under the steps.

2 / THE BOOK

The dark gray clouds were thick like gravy over Cook, Tennessee, and the sun didn't look like it was going to poke itself through them all day. Folks in the small northwestern town of about 250 people had their wood stoves burning, trying to keep warm on the unusually cold and dreary Saturday. Robert and his daddy decided it was a good day to load up the old truck with logs and make a haul to Herndon, a town to the west with about ten times the number of people, where the demand would be high and the money would be, too. Mama D was going to ride along and visit her kinfolk.

While Becky suckled on her left breast, Annie fixed breakfast with her free hand like she did day after day. Raising the children was entirely up to her; no one ever offered to change a diaper, bathe a child or lift a hand in any way except to slap her. They expected eggs, bacon, grits and baking powder biscuits every morning. Sometimes Mama D would buy sausage, but the Barton men loved their crisp bacon.

One-handed Annie had the breakfast preparations down to a science, and the size of the portions never varied: six pieces of bacon and four eggs each for Robert and his daddy. Three pieces of bacon and two eggs for Mama D, and one egg and one piece of bacon each for herself and the boys. The eggs had to be fried in the bacon grease with no broken yolks, and Mama D was always served first, then Robert and Daddy Jack. Annie and the kids ate last. If a yolk ran, it was Annie's to eat, which was fine with her. It was not the happiest meal of the day, for the Bartons were grumpy people. But the anticipation of making some unexpected extra money made her husband and his parents more tolerable on this cool morning, and even Annie had a little zip in her step just knowing they'd be gone all day.

"Don't be lettin' those young-uns from their chores while we're gone," warned Daddy Jack. "It ain't *that* cold outside. Wood gotta be stacked. Chickens gotta eat or we don't."

"Yessir," replied Annie, sliding four perfect sunny-side-up eggs onto his plate.

"And stay away from that Verneice whore," said Mama D. "Townfolk are all talkin' about her bein' a witch or somethang. No need to meddle in her devil voodoo and war paint."

Verneice Stokes was no devil worshiper and no whore, thought Annie, but she didn't dare say anything back to Mama D. Last time she stood up for Verneice, she got the palm of Mama D's hand across her face. Mama D didn't like Verneice because one day Daddy Jack said, "You know, that Verneice ain't a bad lookin' woman." But Annie wondered if her hatred for the neighbor had to do with something more.

She lived two houses down from the Barton family with her mother, Maydell, in a clean home with white aluminum siding. Her daddy died one winter of TB, and when Maydell hadn't been seen for weeks, rumors spread that she'd gone crazy.

Verneice sold cosmetics door-to-door and had lots of women parties at her house. Some say the whiskey she served at her gatherings made the ladies want to spend more money on makeup and perfume. Others say she put a spell on them because they never seemed quite the same after attending one of her parties.

Annie was intrigued by Verneice, who wore pretty clothes and dangling earrings, and piled her hair high in curls atop her head. Lace curtains covered her windows, and she drove a little white sports car.

By seven-thirty, the old truck was pulling away from the Barton house with Robert behind the wheel and Daddy Jack and Mama D sitting in the front seat like the king and queen of Cook. The boys, Will and Dwayne, were still sleeping. Annie tried putting Becky down in her bed, but she fussed, so she tied the baby around her middle torso with a twin sheet and started cleaning the kitchen.

She poured the bacon grease into an empty coffee can to use again later, and then soaked the crusted yoked plates in the sink while she wiped off the table.

Life could be wurse. I could be haulin' in water from the well to warsh dishes like Mama had to do.

The Bartons had running water in the kitchen, but they still had an outhouse and indoor pee closet. As far as she knew, her own daddy still didn't have indoor plumbing in his house or running water in the kitchen sink. Annie felt sorry for his new wife, Loretta.

Loretta Sachett was only two years older than Annie when she married Annie's daddy last fall. At 19, Loretta was pretty old by Cook's standards to be single, and word around town was that the marriage had been "arranged," just like Annie's had been. Loretta was not a pretty girl, Annie remembered, and a lot of people said she was meaner than a wart hog, but her daddy made whiskey, some say better than Uncle Deek. Now Annie's daddy got free whiskey, and maybe even a share of the profits. She wasn't sure.

Annie worried about her eight brothers who were being raised by the likes of Loretta. She hadn't seen any of the boys since she married Robert. They lived up in the hills in an old house that wasn't fit for rats to live in, and she wondered what kind of heathens they were growing up to be with a drunk daddy, a mean stepmother and a filthy home. She imagined her own three children living that kind of life and the thought made her stomach queasy.

While drying the breakfast dishes, Annie glanced out the kitchen window toward Verneice's house and saw her sweeping her front porch. *That porch has gotta be the cleanest in Cook. She's always out thar sweepin'.* When she saw Verneice move to sweep the steps, Annie braced herself on the sink's counter and thought of the book she had found earlier that morning and thrown under her own steps.

"I gotta get that thang outta there!" she cried. "No tellin' whut words or pictures are inside it!"

She looked down at her sleeping baby wrapped around her body and removed her from the sheet and carried her to the crib. She tiptoed to the next room to peek in on the boys and they were sleeping, too. Then she made a mad dash for the back door.

First, she looked around to see if anyone was watching from either side of the house. She got down on her hands and knees and reached under the steps and felt the hardness of the book's cover. Out of nowhere, a cool wind came up from behind her and blew her robe up around her waist. Startled, she grabbed the book with one hand as fast as she could and pulled her robe down with the other. Then she turned around and sat on the bottom step to examine the book up close.

Annie was puzzled, yet relieved, to see that the thick gray book had no title.

"I thought all books had a name," she whispered as she opened the book to the first page. The second page was blank, too. And the third. She fanned through the entire book with her thumb and found that *every* page was empty of words.

"This here's a diary," she said. "A book to write in!"

How funny, she thought, that a book like this would come her way when she couldn't even write. "A diary!" she laughed. *A stupid diary! Ain't that a hoot. I can't even read. How am I gonna write in this thang?*

"Mama, watcha doin' out here?"

Annie jumped up and whirled around to face Dwayne who was standing at the back door. "Dwayne!" she shouted. "Good Lord, you scared the pee out of me!"

"I'm sorry, Mama," he said, rubbing his eyes. "Whut's that?"

Dwayne pointed to the book lying on the steps. Annie fumbled for words. "Oh, that? That ain't nothin'," she replied. "Just an ol' book. Now get back inside. Get yore brother up and let's eat breakfust."

While Dwayne was in his room rustling his brother from the bed, Annie put the book back under the steps.

Later. I'll take this back to the crick later.

3 / THE CLOUD

The animals were acting funny. Rusty, a scruffy old hound that followed Robert home from the woods last year where he had been hunting squirrel, wouldn't come out from under the house for nothing, not even food. The chickens sat motionless, not getting up to eat or even peck at the food that Annie held to their beaks in her cupped hand. The pigs ate, but slow and quiet, all the time rolling their eyes around like somebody was watching them or like they suspected they were getting ready for slaughter. Two birds who appeared to be drunk from eating pokeweed berries shot out suddenly from opposite sides of a tree and flew smack dab into each other, crashing and landing on the barn's roof.

This cold weather has 'em spooked, thought Annie, gazing at the gray, swirling clouds that were moving faster than she'd ever seen before. "Dwayne!" she shouted to her oldest son who was throwing rocks at a dishpan hanging on the tree. "Reach under thar and yank at Rusty. See if he'n alive."

Dwayne crawled under the house and within seconds Rusty was whimpering. "Get up, pup!" Dwayne shouted. The dog didn't budge. "He ain't comin,' Mama!" he shouted back.

"Okay, just let 'em be then. Let's go inside whar it's warm. Can't make a critter eat. Ain't nuthin' we can do. Ain't nuthin' we done wrong. C'mon, Will!" she screamed at her other boy.

Will came around from the back of the barn carrying a large piece of wood to place near the back door. He could hardly walk with his stubby little arms clutching the heavy log, and his breath was heavy with each step. As long as Annie could remember, Will had been strong. When he was born he'd latch his fingers around Annie's finger so tight she'd have to pry them off one by one. He sat up in no time flat and walked before he was a year old. It didn't seem like he was ever a baby. Just three years old, he was tougher than nails, unlike his older brother, Dwayne, who was a weakling.

The boys didn't look like kin either. Dwayne favored Annie with his blond hair and blue eyes, small nose and thin lips. Will was darker with larger features and cheekbones that rose so high that when he smiled, his eyes squinted like a Chinaman. She suspected from the time she laid eyes on Will that he might be Daddy Jack's.

Dwayne was three months old the first time Daddy Jack put his thing inside her. Robert was drunk and passed out on the couch. He and Daddy Jack had paid a visit to Uncle Deek's earlier that night and then went to Buster Jones' house and drank some more. Mama D was spending the night in Herndon with her sister, Helen, whose daughter was birthing in the bed.

Daddy Jack smelled like whiskey and tobacco and was breathing loud when he came into Annie's room that first time. Dwayne was asleep on her chest and Daddy Jack nearly killed the baby when he fell over in the bed on top of her. He picked up Dwayne and put him in the crib, then pulled back the covers and tore off her nightclothes. "This here ain't nobody's bidness but yern and mine," he said as he unzipped his pants. "When you bedded my boy, you got me, too." Then he laughed and started humping.

Annie ran out of nightclothes after his third visit to her bed and, from then on, she wore nothing on the nights when Robert was passed out. She started early morning creek baths to clean Daddy Jack's stench from her body. Then her stomach swelled up again with a baby and she just knew it was his. Will was born when Dwayne turned a year old.

Once when she was sweeping the barn he grabbed her from behind and threw her down on the wooden floor. Strapped to the barn's floor by his weight, Annie tried to pretend it wasn't happening by concentrating on the wasps swarming around their nest in the corner of the barn's ceiling.

I wish I wuz a wasp, she thought, fighting back tears as her body was being violated. *I'd fly down and sting Daddy Jack over an' over an' over, then get all my wasp friends to sting him, too. Then his body would be all puffed up from stings like the drowned puppy in the crick last year. Blood would be runnin' down his eyes and out his ears. Then ol' Doc Wilks would have to cut Daddy Jack's ding-dong off.*

But it never happened. A week later he was at it again. This time he took her and the kids for a ride and stopped along a wooded road where he grabbed her off the seat and bent her over like a dog behind the trees as she listened to the cries from her children locked in the truck. While he was riding her, she imagined a big blackbird swooping down from the sky and pecking him in the head and making him fall over on his back. Then all the blackbirds' friends would come and peck at his ding-dong and that's how the townsfolk would find him – his pecker pecked off.

Mama D suspected something was fishy after that trip to the woods. After all, Annie was *never* allowed to leave the house, not even to talk to neighbors over the fence or sit on the porch. It was odd that Daddy Jack would take Annie somewhere. But Robert never said a word about anything his daddy did and never asked any questions, either. After Becky was born, though, Daddy Jack quit humping her. She guessed that Mama D and Robert had something to do with that.

She didn't give it to him willingly, but Daddy Jack getting what he wanted from her made him act better toward her. And once he stopped, things got pretty mean around the house. He went from humping to hitting, and the bruises were harder to hide than his stench. Robert grabbed her jaw one day and said, "How'd you got that black mark?" Annie wrestled from his grip and said, "I done tripped on yore boots and hit the floor." Robert seemed satisfied with that.

And so with the Barton clan on their way to Herndon to sell wood, Annie could enjoy her children. They loved their mama. When they were all hers, they'd laugh and cuddle. When Robert or his parents were around, they never said a word unless spoken to. Even eight-month-old Becky knew when to stay quiet.

While all three napped in their beds, Annie took the book back to the creek. *I don't want nuthin' to do with this thang. Nuthin' brings nuthin', and I can't take no more hittin'.*

She approached the bank and flung the book into the water with no hesitation. But instead of watching it travel downstream, Annie stood in amazement as the book swirled around and around in front of her like a tornado. A white cloud as tall as the trees rose up from the center of the swirling water. She stood motionless while staring at the billowing cloud, but it wasn't swirling like the tornado she had seen last spring that cut a path through the schoolyard in front of her house. This wasn't gray and ugly like the funnel cloud that picked up the school's swing set and dropped it on Mrs. Tillet's milk cow down the road.

She gasped at the mushroom-like stalk that sprang up from the swirling water. At the top, large fluffy clouds like marshmallows rolled over and over and over. She tried to take a step forward to get a closer look, but her body wouldn't move.

"This time I'm ah' *really* gonna turn to salt!" she cried, remembering how she felt earlier that morning.

A bright light began flickering at the bottom of the stalk and slowly trickled its way upward, stopping at the top of the marshmallow pillow and igniting into a ball like the sun.

"My stars!" exclaimed Annie. "*This* is beautiful!"

Within seconds, the luminous ball revealed the gentle face of a woman. Annie's eyes squinted from the brightness that encircled the face, painfully trying to make out the woman's identity. Confused but not at all afraid, Annie thought that the woman was either Jesus' mother or the beautiful lady in the long flowing gown from the movie star magazine.

The lady's eyes stared back and pierced Annie's as if they were penetrating her soul, and Annie sensed something eerily familiar about them, like she had stared into those eyes before.

4 / THE DEAL

"Somethun's gotta be done 'bout Annie," said Mama D during the ride home from Herndon. "She can't be havin' all these young-uns. We gotta git her fixed."

Robert stared straight ahead at the two-lane highway and didn't say a word. He suspected Mama D knew the two youngest children resembled Daddy Jack. *It would be wurse if Daddy Jack was my real paw, but he ain't*, Robert thought to himself.

Robert's real daddy was killed nearly 20 years earlier in a car accident just outside of Cook. A gas pain in Robert's gut made him flinch behind the wheel as he thought of the story of his father's death that he'd heard over and over and over his entire life.

He'd been told how his daddy, Minner Brown, was driving his new Hudson over to his best friend's house in Herndon to show it off. He had purchased the green four-door just the day before from a dealer in Memphis. Business had been good that year at his gas station, Tinker's Tow & Garage, which he owned and operated in Cook, so he rewarded himself and his growing family with the new vehicle.

Mama D, who married Minner when she was 14, wanted to ride along, but two-year-old Robert had a cough and runny nose, so Minner left them behind, vowing to be back in a few hours.

The day was perfect: Seventy-two degrees, a mild breeze and a snazzy car. What more could a man from Cook want? He passed lots of houses of friends and relatives along the two-lane tarred road to Herndon, and he'd slow down and honk in front of every one of them. Some would come running out of their screen doors waving and shouting, "Take us for a ride!" and Minner would step on the gas and speed away.

There was no passing on that two-lane road – *ever*. The dangerous hills that cropped up every quarter-mile or so blinded drivers from seeing approaching traffic on the other side of the road. A couple of the hills were pretty steep and, if you let your imagination run a little, you could imagine falling off the earth after you rounded the top. It just looked like there was nothing on the other side but sky. One year a whole family – mother, father and four kids — died after hitting a car head-on at the top of one of those hills. The man in the other car died, too.

"No, siree! It just don't pay to take chances on that road," Minner used to say a lot, and the whole county knew it, too.

Minner was one of the first to arrive at the scene of that gruesome head-on collision that killed those seven people. He and Doc Wilks were sitting on the grocery store's front porch playing checkers when the Drummond boy came running down the hill toward them. His feet were moving so fast that his hair and cheeks were slicked back as tight as a cowlick combed with lard. (At least, that's how they both described him later in story-after-story of the accident.)

"Doc Wilks! Doc Wilks!" the Drummond boy shouted, falling to the ground panting. "You gotta come quick! Thar's dead people all over the tarred road on the hill near the Gibbs' shack."

Minner jumped into Doc's truck and Doc picked up the boy and told him to get in the front seat, too. Doc drove to Tinker's and let Minner out to fire up his ambulance. The vehicle's siren was like an air raid signal alerting the whole town that something was wrong. With Doc following behind him, Minner sped toward the accident site in his red emergency vehicle, and a long stream of cars with curious people trailed Doc's truck.

Ethelyn Gibbs, Cook's only Negro midwife, was standing by the side of the road waving a handkerchief at the ambulance with one hand and wiping her eyes with another. All six of her kids had fastened themselves to her body, and three of them were not even visible behind her huge torso. She sobbed and waved the handkerchief in the direction of the accident.

The family involved in the crash was on its way to Cook to visit relatives. Their car was packed with lots of clothes and the trunk burst open upon impact, exploding suitcases all over the road. All seven bodies were thrown from the two vehicles, and it was hard to see where they were lying because all their belongings were strewn everywhere.

After arriving on the scene, Minner was concerned about having only two cots in his ambulance, but it really didn't seem to matter in the end. All of them were dead, so he placed the mother on one cot and put a child under each arm. He put the father on the second cot and the remaining two babies on top of him. One of the boys looked to be the size of his own son, and he began to weep.

The man who was driving the other car was a salesman from Herndon, so everyone realized that neither driver knew the consequences of passing on those hills or traveling too close to the striped line. And there were no witnesses, either. Ethelyn's place was in eye's range, but she said she didn't see anything and neither did her children. But that's what Minner would have expected her to say even if she *had* seen anything. All the occupants were white, and Ethelyn knew there would be hell to pay if she fingered either driver.

Minner placed the dead man from Herndon on the ambulance's floor between the two cots and somberly drove them to Herndon's morgue.

No, there was no passing on these hills. Minner knew that firsthand. He had told everyone that the images of that awful day always crept into his thoughts whenever he approached the Negro shack where Cornelius and Ethelyn Gibbs lived.

So on that beautiful spring day in 1940 behind the wheel of his snazzy new Hudson, Robert's daddy didn't budge from behind the slow logging truck that was in front of him. The bed of long oak was stacked at least five feet high on the flatbed trailer and was held together with two, thick silver chains. The truck's plates were from Arkansas, and the driver stuck his arm out several times motioning Minner to come around him. But, of course, Minner didn't pass him.

As the two vehicles approached the steepest hill on that tarred road, Minner noticed several logs coming loose on the truck's bed. "Holy smokes," he must have said to himself, for that was his favorite saying.

Several logs slid off and slammed into his windshield, decapitating him.

Minner's best friend, Daddy Jack, was a pallbearer and so was Doc Wilks. Shortly after his death, Mama D, then 19, "took a mean spell," as Cook residents say, and was sometimes just downright nasty. Tinker's Tow & Garage had to be sold to pay off the Hudson, and the house had to go to pay for the funeral and Minner's debts Mama D didn't even know he had. Land that Minner's family had had for generations was still Mama D's and was profitable with beans, corn, cotton and pecan trees. Daddy Jack started handling things for Mama D right after Minner's funeral, and a year later they were married.

Mama D didn't *have* to marry Daddy Jack, but the pickings were slim in Cook for a young woman who had a small boy to raise. Besides that, no man wanted a mean, nasty woman as his wife, except Jack, who many suspected was a virgin.

A rabbit shot out from the side of the road and Robert swerved the truck to avoid it, smashing him up against his mama who hung onto his arm. His thoughts returned to the present, and the dilemma his family was now facing.

Maw's right 'bout Annie gettin' fixed, he thought. *Thar's only so much money comin' from the fields. Last year that dadgum bean crop didn't bring in a dime. Who knows? The way the crazy weather is actin,' it might be the dadgum cotton next.*

Mama D patted Robert's hand that was gripping the steering wheel. "Ol' Doc Wilks can fix her. He's been a'wantin' that patch of land down by the crick since you wuz a baby. I think we can work somethin' out with him to doctor her up. Lord knows we need that girl to cook and clean."

Daddy Jack piped up. "And whut about the young-uns? We don't know piss 'bout takin' care of 'em, and you know she won't be right healthy to lift 'em or tend to 'em if she gits cut on."

The truck was silent. That was true, they all thought. Annie was the only one who took care of the children. She nursed little Becky, changed diapers, cleaned up their messes, cooked everyone's meals, washed clothes.

"Now, Jack. You know good how she up and took care of the boys an hour after birthin' Becky," explained Mama D. "That girl is strong. 'Member that time she fell and Doc Wilks sewed her head? Didn't slow her down none."

"I don't know, Maw," said Robert, now realizing the seriousness of the surgery. "Cuttin' on her stomach's gotta make her sicker. Maybe if we don't do *it* so much it won't take."

Mama D took in a big gulp of air into her lungs. "It's not *you* that frets me so, son," she snapped.

Daddy Jack squirmed in his seat and looked out the window at the trees that lined the highway. Robert just stared straight ahead at the road. Her heavy breathing was all that was heard in the car for miles.

Then Robert spoke up. "Okay," he sighed. "I know whar the papers are to that land. Let's go see Doc."

Doc Wilks was a nice man whose wife, Martha, ruled the roost. "Henpecked" was how people best described him. He had an examining room and office in his home up the hill from the Bartons' so Martha could keep a watchful eye on him. She never liked the young pregnant girls who came to see him, and often accused her husband of examining them too much.

In his heyday, Doc took care of all the townsfolk, bringing their babies into the world, sewing up wounds, and administering medicine for all the colds and flu that plagued Cook's residents.

There wasn't anyone in Cook Doc hadn't helped, except for the Negroes who relied solely on Ethelyn Gibbs' home remedies and birthing skills. Even Annie had a history with Doc. When she was five years old, Doc saved her daddy's life.

Annie's daddy, Ernest Slayton, hadn't ever worked for a logging company before, but when word got around that temporary workers were needed to clear land for a major road, Annie's mama made him join up. He lied and said he'd done that kind of work before, so they hired him. It was the best money her daddy had ever made, and it turned out to be the last decent job he would *ever* have.

While clearing some land, a tree fell right in front of him, shaving his nose and plummeting right down on his left foot. Doc Wilks had to cut half of his foot off. His spirit broke after that and people gawked and whispered when they saw him, calling him a "drunken cripple." That was when Annie's mother started taking in ironing and darning, and Annie and her brothers had to pick cotton for extra money. Life for the Slayton family was always a struggle, but more so after her daddy's injury.

Over the past 10 years, though, Doc had slowed down some. His short-term memory was fading. He talked a lot about the past but couldn't remember simple things like wearing underwear, buckling his belt and matching his socks. At first, Martha thought he had left his underwear somewhere else when she noticed that he didn't have any on while he was undressing for bed one night. He was the talk of the town when she booted him out and locked him out of the house for two days. The grocer, Clyde Tubbs, called her one night when he found Doc sleeping on the porch of his store. That's when she knew he had no place to go and there was no other woman. She took him home and cleaned him up.

"William Wilks," she scolded, "you're just not right in the head anymore."

Since then, she had dressed and undressed him every day. On some days she had to tell him who she was and what he was supposed to be doing. On other days, he was sharp as a tack. It didn't take long before word got around that ol' Doc Wilks was losing his mind and people stopped coming to him for help. But right now, he was the Bartons' only hope for stopping Annie from having babies because they had no money to pay a doctor in Herndon.

As the Bartons' truck rolled into Doc's driveway, the old man got up from the porch's swing and walked down the steps.

"Hey!" he hollered to them. "How are y'all doin'?"

"Fine, just fine," answered Daddy Jack, climbing out of the truck. "Are we catchin' y'all at a bad time?"

"Naw, c'mon in," he said, motioning with his hands.

And there, in the beautiful new kitchen that Martha Wilks had just had remodeled, the Bartons plotted out their scheme to sterilize Annie.

"Friday looks good for me," said Doc.

"Friday it is," said Daddy Jack, sealing the deal with a handshake.

5 / THE SETTING

Annie opened her eyes and stared at the clump of weeds on the ground next to her. She smiled, closed her eyes again and rustled in the soft earth, stretching, yawning and rolling onto her back. While looking up to the sky, she realized the sun was low and there was a faint twinkling of stars.

She sat up slowly and began dusting the grass and dirt from her legs and arms. She could hear the peaceful flow of the creek, the swishing of the trees overhead and a mockingbird somewhere in the distance. She looked behind her at the house and tried to recall what led her to the creek's bank. Her head was foggy like she'd just awakened from a deep sleep and her sight was blurry. She squinted to see clearly. Within seconds her eyes shot wide open and she was on her feet running toward the house where she'd left her children in their beds.

Her heart pounded faster and faster with each footprint that crushed the ground in front of her, and a sudden weakness took over her entire body. She almost fainted at the thought of Robert and his parents returning from their trip and finding the children alone in the house.

"Oh, dear God," she cried, please don't let Robert be home yet! And please, please, please, pleeeeeese let my babies be safe!"

She flung open the screen door with such force that it almost came off its hinges. Then she grabbed the knob to the kitchen door, opened it and flipped on the light. There was no sound except her panting. Weak-kneed, she stumbled to the boys' room and turned on the light. Dwayne and Will were snuggled together asleep. Through the curtains she saw car lights pulling up alongside the house.

"Dwayne! Time to get up!" she shouted. "Git yore brother up now."

She darted to her bedroom and scooped up Becky from her crib. "Y'all need to act like we ain't been lazy cuz yer daddy's home and he won't take to us layin' 'round," she said in a loud whisper to the boys. Two doors slammed outside and she was relieved to hear the Bartons' footsteps on the front porch because usually they entered the house through the rear. She scurried the boys out to the back porch and grabbed two ears of corn from a basket and put one in each of their hands. "Here!" she cried. "Act like y'all been shuckin' corn!"

She was changing Becky's diaper when the front door opened.

"Girl?" Mama D shouted. "Girl, where you be?"

Annie showed herself in the kitchen doorway that led to the living room. Becky was suckling on her breast.

"Fix us some tea," she ordered.

Daddy Jack went straight to the bedroom to get a swig of whiskey from a bottle he kept in an old coat that was hanging on a hook inside the closet. Annie knew exactly where he was going because she discovered the bottle one day when she was leaning over to pick up the dirty clothes off the floor. When she stood up, the bottle hit her head and left a welt. One afternoon while alone in the house she got a bright idea to seek a little revenge on Daddy Jack. She went out to the well and scraped some dried bird droppings off its roof and ground it up to a fine dust. Then she sprinkled the bird shit into his whiskey bottle. That night when he came home, he went for his usual swig and came running out of the bedroom spitting, coughing and grabbing his throat. Annie had to run outside so her laughter wouldn't be heard. Mama D was scolding him for smoking too many cigarettes at Uncle Deek's.

She ain't got a spoonful of sense, thought Annie while preparing tea for Mama D and Daddy Jack, wishing she had kept some of that ground bird shit to put in their tea.

Robert walked in the front door and made a beeline for the back door to get to the outhouse, stepping over the boys without saying a word. Dwayne and Will brought corn into the kitchen and Annie prepared a large pot on the stove to cook it in. Then she grabbed three skinned squirrels from the refrigerator, soaked all the parts in egg and dredged them in flour. She scooped two spoons of lard into a frying pan and began frying the meat. Supper was starting to take shape, and Annie asked the boys to help her set the table.

"Set the fork on this side of the plate and the knife on the other, with the sharp side facin' the plate," Annie instructed. "The spoons go on the outside of the knife, and the napkin goes here."

The boys did as she ordered but glanced at each other as they rounded the table, placing the utensils exactly where she said to put them, and wondering why it all mattered now. Robert came in the back door, looked at the table and started yelling.

"Whut the hell is goin' on, Annie? Why you have these young-uns put knifes and spoons out? And whut's this? A napkin? Get this here sissy thang off and get me my towel!"

Mama D heard the ruckus and came into the kitchen. She scanned the room and eyed the place settings. "Girl, I guess you like dish warshin.' That's all I can figure. Or you been talkin' to that Verneice woman and she been tellin' you some different ways," she said, shaking her head back and forth. "This here ain't nuthin' but blame foolishness to me. And what's this?" she said, picking up a napkin and dangling it. "Ain't these my Maw's?"

Robert grabbed Becky from Annie's arm and set her on the floor. Then he took Annie's arms and lifted her up until her face met his. Each word from his mouth spit on her eyes and nose.

"Whut have we done told you 'bout that witch? YOU STAY AWAY FROM HER!" he shouted.

He let go and dropped her to the floor. Becky started crying and the boys took off to their room. Annie stood up and didn't say a word. She walked slowly over to the stove to turn the meat as if nothing had happened. Robert stomped out to join his parents in the living room. She was alone in the kitchen now, except for Becky, and she could finish cooking. She knew there was no way Robert was going to hit her and send her away until supper was on the table and his fat face was chewing squirrel.

That night Annie couldn't sleep, her mind reeling from the supper fight. Why had she told the boys to put all those things on the table? She hadn't talked to Verneice in two forevers, she thought. And the meal – it was the best she'd ever cooked. Mashed potatoes, cream gravy, corn-on-the-cob, fried squirrel and fresh onions and radishes from the garden. The Bartons lapped it all up, not leaving a speck of leftovers.

"This cool weather done made yore brain grow or somethang," quipped Mama D at the supper table. "It's like some light done gone off in yore head and smarted you up with the vittles."

Yes, Annie thought later when she was in bed. *There was a light. A bright light. But wuz it in my head?*

6 / THE DAISIES

Annie awoke the next morning and quietly tiptoed to the pee closet off the kitchen to relieve herself in the stainless steel pan. Their home, according to Mama D's rantings, was the only one in Cook that still had an outhouse and a pee pot inside.

"No one else's house smells like pee 'cept ours!" she screamed one morning after spilling the urine-filled pan onto the linoleum floor. "My granddaddy helped build Cook and we'n the last to be civilized folk! Girl! Get in here and clean up this shit."

The pee closet didn't have a door, just a white curtain made from a sheet that slid back and forth on an old curtain rod. Annie wondered what it would be like to sit on a toilet seat and hear water sucking her pee and doo-doo away. Verneice had a brand new bathroom with a tub that sank into the ground. Annie heard her tell Mama D about it one day when she was walking past the house. Mama D was sitting in the swing on the front porch and Verneice just started talking to her like they were old friends.

"Why, lord-a-mercy! Hey there, Mis' Barton!" Verneice had yelled. "Did y'all see that plumbing truck run by here yesterday? Yeah, Mama and me got us a new bathroom. They call the tile color 'champagne.' Imagine that! And the tub fits three people and is low in the ground. It's like somethin' off the pages of *Good Housekeeping*. You truly don't know what you're missin'."

"Fits three people, does it?" asked Mama D. "And just how you knowed that?"

Verneice put her left hand on her hip, cocked her head to one side and twirled her lime green purse with her other hand. "Why, me and Mama and that cute little ol' plumber filled that deep tub up with bubble bath and got naked and jumped in! That's how I know!" Then she threw back her head and laughed.

Mama D gasped. "Yore nothin' but ah whore, Verneice," she shouted.

"Oh, yeah?" Verneice screamed back. "Well, you're nothin' but a low-down, good-for-nothing piece of trash that treats your dog better'n you treat your own kin." She took a deep breath and put her hands on each hip and said, "And you know what?"

"Whut?" Mama D asked sternly.

"I'd keep my eyes on that old man of yours. He looks like he needs a good scrubbin'."

Then she turned on her high heels and walked down the road, swaying prissy-like in her tight pants and swinging her purse back and forth. Her teased, lacquered hair didn't budge in the breeze, but her dangling earrings clanked together like wind chimes. Her laughter ruffled Mama D's feathers and caused her face to puff up and turn red.

Mama D leaped from the swing, stomped into the house, slammed the front door and grabbed Annie's arm as she was running away from the window.

"Girl, if I *ev'r* see you talkin' to that tramp, I'll kill you!" she screamed, her rotten breath smelling up Annie's hair. Then she threw Annie down on the couch and went to her bedroom.

Annie held back a smirk, awed by Verneice's boldness. She wished she could say something – *anything* – like that to get Mama D's goat, but nothing ever came out of her mouth. She wanted to be like Verneice, highfalutin ways, stiff hair and all.

Instead of going directly down to the creek for her morning bath, Annie decided to make a cup of tea. While striking the match to light the burner under the kettle, she thought about the book.

Where'd I leave that dang thang? she thought, scratching her head. *Didn't I throw it in the crick?*

The teapot whistled softly and Annie took it off the stove quickly so no one would wake up. She walked quietly out of the house, teacup in hand, toward the creek where she slowly sipped the brew and breathed in the crisp morning air. While sitting on the creek's bank, she closed her eyes and felt the breeze blow through her hair and its freshness creep into her skin. She thought about the lady in the long flowing gown, this time wearing makeup that Verneice had sold to her. She sniffed the sweet honeysuckle from a nearby bush and imagined smelling that way all over — her hair, her clothes, her skin. She closed her eyes and daydreamed about the man in the black suit, this time kissing the sweet skin on her honeysuckled neck and whispering in her ear over and over between each suck of his lips, *"Annie Louise, I love you. I love you. I love you."*

She opened her eyes and took in the beauty of Pig Dog Creek. Little critters rustled along the bank and in the trees. Two squirrels chased each other around and around a tree trunk, and five featherless baby birds awaited their breakfast in a nest with their necks stretched high and their mouths opened wide to the sky. A few white cranes walked along the water's edge and a turtle crawled up onto a tree stump in the middle of the water.

Her tea was gone and the cup was cold. Annie stood up to go back to the house when she noticed the book beside her.

"There it is!" she said aloud. "It done floated back!"

But the book was dry and dusty. A strong gust of wind blew it open and the pages flipped. She saw pictures flip by, but thought she must be seeing things because the last time she looked at it all the pages were blank. Puzzled, she picked it up and drew it close to her eyes.

On the first five pages were pictures of kitchen tables. The first table was white and round with four plates decorated with daisies. A small orange rug was under each plate. The forks were placed on the left, and the knives and spoons were on the right. Two cute little salt and pepper shakers shaped like tomatoes sat in the middle of the table with a basket of yellow napkins.

On the next page was a wooden table with white doilies under the plates that had matching cups and saucers. A beautiful jar of yellow and pink flowers sat in the middle of the table, and at the right of each plate was a stemmed glass with pink water in it. Pink pleated, ironed napkins were to the left of the forks.

They were the only pages that were filled with pictures. The rest were empty. "Maybe I didn't see these before," she said, scratching her head. "Or maybe I did and disremembered."

There were numerous table settings, some with striped tablecloths, some with checked tops, and even wooden coffee tables set with silver kettles and teacups. Candles, flowers, plaster animals and ivy plants decorated the tables with beauty Annie had never seen before, not even in the movie magazine.

"I knowed I didn't see these before," Annie said. *But I must have*, she thought, remembering how she told her boys to set the table the night before.

The old rooster crowed from the top of the hen house and she knew it was time to fix breakfast.

"Dang!" she said, looking at the book. "Dang! Whut am a'gonna do with this thang?"

Her eyes scanned the creek's bank looking for a safe place for the book when she spotted a hollow log. She gently placed it inside, about halfway down.

"There," she said, patting the cover of the book as if it was alive. "I'll be back t'mara." Then she found a large rock to place in front of the log's opening. On the way back to the house, she stopped to pick some wild daisies that were growing alongside the barn.

"Hmmmmmm …. these'll look good in a jar of water," she said.

And the flowers were sitting in the middle of her beautifully set table when the Bartons came into the kitchen for breakfast.

7 / THE EMERGENCY

Robert took one look at the table and lunged at Annie's neck with both hands. Mama D and Daddy Jack stood frozen with their mouths open, looking at the table settings first, then at Robert with his hands wringing Annie's throat, then back at the table. Dwayne cried and pulled at his daddy's pants.

"Whut in the name of Hell is wrong with you, girl?" Robert yelled, forcing her to the kitchen floor. "Didn't I tell you to stop tawkin' to that Verneice whore?"

Mama D butted in. "Stop, Robert!" she yelled. "Stop right now!"

Robert eased his grip on Annie and turned toward his mother. His face was beet red and veins were popping out of his neck, throbbing like a turkey. "Stop?" he yelled back. "*Stop?* Since when you side with Annie?"

"Shhhhh…" she said in a quiet voice. "I ain't shore, but I think somebuddy's at the front door."

The house fell quiet and they all listened closely. The knock was louder the second time. Robert let go of Annie and stood up. "Good God, Maw," he said. "Who you think it is?"

Daddy Jack piped up, "Waal, I'll just go see."

Annie got up and fixed her dress and crumpled apron, straightening the wrinkled cotton, then pushing back the strands of hair that had come loose from her ponytail. She put her arms around Dwayne who had stopped crying now, and she could hear Daddy Jack and another man's voice at the front door. Their voices got louder as they approached the kitchen, and Annie went about her business putting food on the table.

"Good morning, y'all," said Sheriff Haynes, his hat in one hand and his eyes on the beautifully set table. "Why, Mis' Annie," he said. "That's a right purdy table you got there."

Annie looked at him and managed a faint smile. She could see Robert through the corner of her eye burning a hole through her.

"Set yersef down, Larry," said Daddy Jack, pulling out a chair for the sheriff. "Have ya some brekfust."

The invitation must have been tempting. On the table was a feast of pancakes, hot syrup, bacon, sausage, scrambled eggs and biscuits. The silverware was carefully arranged around each plate, and a folded cloth napkin was on each side. The daisies added much-needed life to the scuffed oak table.

"Naw," Sheriff Haynes replied. "I'm afraid this ain't a social visit. Annie, you and the kids might want to leave the room while I talk to your kinfolk. It ain't pretty talk for yer young-uns to hear."

Annie quickly gathered up the boys and shooed them outside to feed the chickens. She peeked in on Becky who was taking her morning nap, then returned to the kitchen. She wasn't about to miss this conversation unless she was ordered to.

"Coffee, Sheriff Haynes?" she asked.

Robert watched her move from the stove to the table where she retrieved a cup and saucer from a place setting and handed it to the sheriff.

"Why, that's mighty nice of you, Annie," he said.

"Cream? Sugar?" she asked.

"No, ma'am," the sheriff replied. "Thank you mighty."

"Fetch us some, too, girl," demanded Mama D. "Let's go in yonder and talk, y'all."

Daddy Jack, Mama D, Robert and Sheriff Haynes went into the living room, leaving Annie alone in the kitchen. She tiptoed to the doorway and could see all four of them in an oval mirror that was hanging over a chair.

"Folks," Sheriff Haynes said, "we've got an ugly problem. The ugliest thang that's happened in Cook since I've lived here."

Mama D looked at Daddy Jack and squirmed in her chair. "I know whut it is," Mama D said, her eyes opened wide and her lips puckered tight. "It's that Verneice woman. She's done run off with somebuddy's man."

Sheriff Haynes scratched his head and chuckled, "No, Dorthea, it's not that simple. I wish it was, but it ain't."

Annie's ears perked up like a jackrabbit. "Dorthea?" Annie whispered. *Dorthea? Whut kinda name is that! I ain't never heered no one call Mama D Dorthea!*

Sheriff Haynes hesitated, then took in a big breath of air and exhaled it slowly before speaking. "Y'all know the Negro family up on the tarred road, Ethelyn and Cornelius Gibbs?"

"Yessir," Mama D said, her eyes growing wider with interest.

"Well," the sheriff continued, "their youngest boy, Calvin, was tarred and feathered last night and tied to a tree behind the church. Someone saw the Drummond boy and his friend Billy cleaning tar off their hands with gasoline early this morning. They ran off into the hills and we're asking everyone to help us catch 'em."

Robert had known Calvin all of his life, as good as any white boy could know a colored in the small town without being looked down upon. Calvin's entire family had worked the Bartons' crops, cleared land, and performed other laborious chores for more than 20 years. The two young men were about the same age, but Calvin was small and sickly. He was Ethelyn's youngest, and the most difficult to bear of all her children. Word around Cook was that Calvin had stayed in the birth canal too long without oxygen.

"Is Calvin alive?" asked Robert.

"Yes, thank God," answered the sheriff. "His mama is all tore up over it, and his daddy ... well ... we had to lock Cornelius up in the jail temporarily because he just went crazy."

"Whut can we do, Larry?" Daddy Jack asked.

"I sure could use y'all to help search the hills, and it'd be a great help if you could bring that old hound of yours," the sheriff replied. "And Dorthea, a heap o' womenfolk are at the preacher's house fixin' food for the family and the men in the hills. We're takin' shifts, so there'll be lots of mouths to feed. I don't have to tell y'all how important it is that we catch those boys," he said. "Cook, Tennessee, ain't gonna look too good if this thang makes the newspapers."

"Count us in," said Daddy Jack.

The sheriff got up to leave. "I knew I could count on y'all. Our next shift goes out in an hour."

"We'll be there," Robert said, shaking the sheriff's hand.

Annie heard the sheriff leave and ran back into the boys' room. She heard Mama D's feet walking on the linoleum floor in the kitchen.

"Girl!" she shouted. "Girl, get in here and pack up this food. We gotta take it with us."

Annie returned to the kitchen and wrapped the breakfast in waxed paper. Daddy Jack and Robert put their hunting boots on and grabbed their rifles. They all left in a huff, without even a good-bye to Annie or the boys or an explanation of where they were going.

She hollered for Dwayne and Will to come into the house and washed them up for breakfast. They didn't ask where their daddy was or what the sheriff wanted. They just ate and went back outside.

Annie cleared the dishes and scrubbed the kitchen from top to bottom. Becky was on the floor on a blanket, rocking back and forth on her hands and knees and jabbering.

"Why, yore about to take off, ain't you, Becky girl?" Annie asked her baby in a sweet, high-pitched voice. "Come here, I'll take you for a spin."

She whisked the baby up into the air and whirled her around the house. Becky giggled as they went from room to room. Annie caught a glimpse of herself in the living room mirror and stopped to take a closer look. Becky beat the mirror with her tiny hand as Annie examined her own image – her hair, her face and her grease-stained dress.

"Good God, I look awful!" she said. "Mama's gonna fix up. Wanna watch?" she said, holding the laughing baby high into the air. "C'mon, let's go to the bedroom."

Becky sat on the bed watching her mother go through a box of clothes Mama D had brought home from her sister's house. They all looked like Helen, ten sizes too big and decorated with fat flowers. But Annie spied a crumpled yellow dress at the bottom of the box that didn't look like it was made from a lot of material. She held it up and smiled at the white lace collar.

"Why, Becky, I do declare! This here's the one," she said. "Mis' Helen done throwed one of her daughter's thangs in here!" Becky clapped her hands together and Annie went to set up the ironing board.

While Becky and the boys were taking their afternoon nap, Annie walked down to the creek to bathe and wash her hair. When she got back to the house, she tore through Mama D's room looking for lipstick or hair curlers that she'd seen Mama D wearing a long time ago. A small tube of pink lipstick was open and melted at the back of one of the drawers, so Annie scraped a little into a spoon to use later. She found six bristle rollers, but only three bobby pins to fasten them into her hair.

"I don't know how to use them thangs anyhow," she said, throwing them back into the drawer. "Guess I'll just let it hang." Then she remembered the flowers on the kitchen table and pinned one in her hair over her ear.

She dotted the lipstick on her cheeks and gently rubbed the color in. She smeared some on her lips, too. She couldn't wait to slip into the yellow cotton dress and surprise the kids. After giving herself a once-over in the mirror, she walked to the boys' room to wake them up.

"Mama?" Dwayne asked, rubbing his eyes to see more clearly. "Mama, is that you?"

"Yep, it's yore mama!" she said, turning around in her dress. "Whut do y'all think?"

Will sat and stared, cocking his head from side-to-side and up and down. When he smiled, Annie knew he approved.

"Mama, whut 'bout Daddy?" Dwayne asked. "He gonna hit you a'gin?"

"Naw," Annie replied. "I'll take it off soon. Say, how 'bout we picknick?"

"Yeah!" the boys shouted in unison.

It was two o'clock when Annie and the kids rolled out their blanket along the creek and spread out their food. The kids didn't eat much because they were too excited about playing in the creek. They weren't normally allowed to even go near the bank. But Annie kept a close eye on them and they swore they wouldn't tell a soul.

Feeling pretty in the yellow dress with her clean hair blowing slightly in the breeze, Annie looked down at her daughter sitting on the blanket and smiled. "We should'a done this a long time ago, baby girl," she said.

They sat there for a few minutes enjoying the beauty of the creek when Annie caught a whiff of Becky's dirty diaper. She leaned over on the blanket and looked into her baby's tiny face that was beet red from straining. "Li'l girl, you got a surprise for yore mama?" she asked.

Becky quit straining and laughed. While Annie was changing the diaper, Becky's face puckered up with fright from her brother's screams.

"Mama! Mama!" Dwayne yelled. "Mama! Mama! Will's hurt!"

Annie flew down to the water's edge, leaving Becky behind on the blanket. "Oh, God, pleese, pleese, pleese let my baby be okay! I should'a never put this dress on. I should'a never put the stuff on my face. I should'a never brung 'em here!"

Will was lying on his stomach, facedown in the water. Annie quickly pulled him over and saw blood oozing from his forehead. He had hit a rock along the creek's edge, but was still breathing.

"Dwayne, go yonder and fetch Mis' Verneice!" she screamed.

The boy stood frozen, staring at the blood running down Will's forehead.

"Go on! Git!" she ordered.

She carried Will up to the blanket where Becky was sitting and put a cloth napkin over the bloody wound. *He is alive, and his head'll heal,* she thought. "He *is* alive, he *is* alive, he *is* alive," she kept saying over and over as she rocked him gently back and forth in her arms.

Verneice and Dwayne were both out of breath when they reached the creek's bank. "I already called Dub's ambulance," Verneice said to Annie. "He's on his way."

The words no sooner spit from her mouth when they heard the siren. The whole town could hear that siren. *All of Cook will know somethin's wrong at our house,* Annie thought.

Dub scooped up Will and put him in the back of his ambulance. "Mis' Annie," he said calmly, "Will's going to be okay, but we have to take him to Herndon. You can ride back there with him."

Herndon? Ride to Herndon? Was Dub crazy? She couldn't go in an ambulance to Herndon!

Dub saw the fear in her eyes. "They won't treat him without a parent to sign the papers," he explained. "If Robert ain't home, then it's gotta be you."

Verneice motioned for her to get into the ambulance. "Go ahead, honey. I'll take Dwayne and Becky to my house until your kin get home. Now go on."

Annie looked at Will lying on the cot, blood soaking through the bandage Dub had put on his head. She hopped in.

The siren blared as they drove through the dirt roads of Cook. Annie patted Will with one hand and held onto a strap on the ambulance's ceiling with the other.

Sign papers? Annie thought. *Sign some papers? Why, I can't even write my name!*

Through the front windshield, Annie could see Dub turning the ambulance onto the tarred road leading out of Cook. The siren was blaring so loud it hurt her ears. People came running out from their houses as it sped down the road, trying to peer into the vehicle to see who was on the cot.

Annie turned toward the two rear doors of the speeding vehicle and looked out the windows. She could see the whole town – the schoolhouse, the grocery store, the old gas station, the church and the different house shapes that dotted the land around them.

It was the first time she'd set her eyes on Cook since she was 12 years old.

8 / THE SWINE

Mama D pulled back the lace curtains in the dining room of the preacher's home and watched the ambulance tear down the road.

"Lordy, Dub's a'goin' fast," she said to the other two ladies who were making sandwiches at the table. "Must be a bad one. Wunder who it is?"

"Maybe they done shot that Drummond boy or his friend," said 93-year-old Emma Lou Parsons, Cook's oldest resident. "I'd hate to think that those white boys risked their own lives just to play a prank on a black boy. What is this world a'comin' to, Dorthea?"

"I don't know," said Mama D, shaking her head. "I just don't know."

The back door to the preacher's house flew open, startling them. They were surprised to see Sheriff Haynes and Robert carrying the Drummond boy through the door. Robert was holding the boy's feet and the sheriff had a good grip under each of his arms. Blood soaked the Drummond boy's shirt and his head slumped forward into the sheriff's arm as they carried him to the bedroom.

"Someone fetch us some warm water," yelled Sheriff Haynes to the ladies. "This boy is hurt bad and there ain't no ambulance to carry him off. We gotta tend to his wounds until Dub gets back. Somebody call Doc Wilks and tell him to get his ass over here."

The ladies scurried in all directions to get water, towels and bandages. Emma Lou called the doctor. Sheriff Haynes and Robert laid the Drummond boy on the bed and unbuttoned his shirt. Mama D brought the water and a dampened cloth around to the side of the bed. She washed the Drummond boy's face and pushed back the brown hair from his brow while the men wrestled with removing his shirt. Mama D and the other ladies stood around the bed, gasping at the open wounds on his chest.

"Who shot 'em up, Larry?" Mama D asked. "Don't tell me it wuz one of my kin."

Sheriff Haynes shook his head back and forth and let out a big laugh. The ladies looked at each other, their mouths opened, surprised at the lawman's lack of respect for the wounded.

The sheriff's chuckle was infectious to Robert, who had to turn his back to the women so they couldn't see his face about to explode with glee.

Mama D was suspicious and sniffed the air for whiskey. She had a good nose for moonshine, and she knew it was on someone's breath.

"Whut in the hell is funny 'bout this boy bein' shot, Larry?" she fumed. "Have y'all been drinkin'?"

Sheriff Haynes looked at Robert and the two of them burst out cackling, spitting and slapping each other on their backs.

"Y'all have!" she screamed.

"No, no, Dorthea. It ain't nothin' like that," the sheriff said, trying to straighten the smirk on his face. "First of all, this here ain't no boy. Andy Drummond is 28 years old, and in my book that's a grown man. And second, '*nobody done shot him up,*' " he said, in a voice mimicking her Tennessee accent. "We had to wrassle a wild boar off his chest that decided to have him for dinner. Those wounds aren't deep, but they do need tendin' to."

Mama D was still confused. "If he ain't hurt bad, why ain't he awake?"

This time it was Robert who broke up laughing. He laughed so hard he farted, and the two ladies in the room made a beeline toward the kitchen. It was a good thing they did, because his fart really stunk up the place. It smelled like rotten eggs, and combined with the whiskey fumes, blood, and boar's spit and snot all over the Drummond boy's clothes, one of those little ladies was going to pass out anyway.

"Maw," he said, gasping for breath and holding his stomach. "The Drummond boy is out cold. He's stinkin' drunk."

"Drunk?" Mama D asked. "I knew I smelled moonshine!"

Sheriff Haynes explained, "You see, Dorthea, we spotted Andy here takin' a leak down by Miller's pond. We saw him set his jug of whiskey down by his feet and out of nowhere this big ol' boar came charging at him!"

Mama D was confused. "Why, I ain't ever heered of no wild boar attackin' a human bean."

"Maw," said Robert. "We thought he was headin' for Andy, too, but he wanted his jug. All of a sudden he grabbed it 'tweenth his teeth and Andy started hollarin' and runnin' after it, then he jumped on that ol' boar and they fought over the damn thang! He wuz an onry ol' cuss, that boar."

The Drummond boy moaned in the bed and Mama D wiped his forehead with a wet rag. "Y'all are story'n" she said. "Ain't heard tell of no wild boar in years."

"It's true, Maw," said Robert. "He wuz the fattest damn boar I ever saw, an' he woulda killed Andy shore thang if Rusty hadn't jumped on him and started bitin' his ears. That scroungy mutt wrassled that ol' boar to the ground and me and the sheriff tried to tie up his feet but he got away."

"What's all this about a boar?" asked Doc Wilks, entering the bedroom. "You say a boar did this to him? And what in Sam Hill is that damned smell?"

"That's right, Doc," said Sheriff Haynes. "The bites ain't too bad, but they sure need some salve or somethin'."

"Where's the other boy? That friend of his. Billy, is it?" Doc asked.

"Jack and Ike took him to the jail," answered the sheriff. "He didn't see a thing. He passed out dead drunk near Miller's pond where Andy was pissin'. How bad does he look, Doc?"

Doc Wilks poked about the Drummond boy's chest and shook his head. "This one don't look good at all," he said, pointing to the hole near the bottom of his rib cage. See how it's deeper than the rest and oozing blood? It'll need stitches for sure. Anytime a wild animal bites a man, he should report it to the authorities and quarantine the animal immediately, because their bites can be deadly. Why, I've seen grown men die from a dog bite. Did either of y'all get bit while you were fightin' this thing off?"

Both men examined their arms for marks. "None on me," said the sheriff.

Robert stared at a red spot on his upper arm, trying to decide if it was old or new.

"What's that, Robert?" asked the doctor.

"Well," said Robert, "I'm tryin' to think if it's from the varmint."

"Let me take a look," said Doc. He walked across the room to Robert and put his fingers on the wound and squeezed it hard. Blood squirted and ran down his arm.

"Ouch!"

"It's from the boar, son."

Mama D dabbed the blood with a wet cloth. "I remember now," said Robert. "I had ah holt of his front legs and he come at me. It made me jump back and then he run off. I didn't know he got me, though. Damn!"

"As soon as Dub gets back from his hospital trip, he'll be taking another one with you and Andy here," said Doc.

"Ah, geez," said Robert. "I ain't ever set foot in that Herndon hospital, *ever!*"

"There's a first time for everything, son," Doc said. "Better to be safe than sorry. Those folks over there know their medicine. Why, I'd trust 'em with my own."

"Okay," Robert replied reluctantly. "Who'd Dub carry to Herndon anyway?"

"Don't know, son," said Doc. "Etta Mae Sawyer swears she saw some blonde-headed woman in the back of the ambulance, but I don't know how she could tell that. You know Dub speeds down that road fast enough to flap the tar."

"Yeah," said Robert. "A blonde lady, huh? Don't know who that could be."

9 / THE HOSPITAL

As soon as the ambulance pulled into the emergency entrance, two young men in white coats and pants opened the back doors of the vehicle and pulled out Will's cot. Annie sat frozen, watching her little boy being carried off by strangers.

"Whar y'all goin' with my boy?" she hollered.

"Just follow us," one of them yelled back.

Annie jumped from the vehicle and ran after the men. When they got inside the double glass doors, one of the men turned to her and said, "You wait right here, ma'am. Someone will be out to have you fill out the paperwork. What's your boy's name?"

"Will," she answered with quivering lips. "His name is Will. He ain't never been apart from his mama, and I need to be with him."

"We'll take good care of him until you fill out the forms, okay, lady?" one of the men said. "Then you can be with your son. But right now we need to take care of his problem. Just have a seat."

Annie's whole body trembled and she had difficulty breathing. Tears welled up in her eyes as she scanned the waiting room for a seat. There was only one empty chair next to an old lady with gray hair and glasses.

"Come and sit here, darlin'," said the old lady, patting the seat of the chair. "It'll be all right. They'll take good care of your boy."

Annie walked over to the chair and sat down, staring straight ahead at the doors where Will's cot had just passed through. A nurse walked up to her and gave her a clipboard and pen.

"Just fill out this form, ma'am, and we can start treating your son," she said, shoving the paperwork at Annie. "Just bring it to me when you're finished. I'll be right behind that window." She pointed to a huge pane of glass with lots of people scurrying around behind it.

Annie's tears dripped from her eyes onto the page of words and blank lines. She sat staring at the blurry paperwork for a few minutes before the old lady spoke up.

"Can I help you, hon?" the old lady asked. "I've got quite a bit of experience filling out these forms. My husband, bless his heart, is carried here twice a week with his diabetes."

Annie looked at the kind woman who was no bigger than the chair she was sitting in. Her eyes glowed with warmth that Annie was unaccustomed to, and her trembling eased. She needed a friend right now and the lady's voice was as soothing as her own mama's. She decided to tell the truth, that she couldn't read or write, and if she didn't fill out the papers, her little boy wouldn't get help.

"Oh, is that all?" the lady asked, after hearing Annie's confession. "We can fix that. Let me have that board and I'll read you the questions and write in the answers for you. Here, take this hankie and wipe those eyes. A pretty girl like you shouldn't be crying."

Annie took the handkerchief and smiled when she saw that it was embroidered with small daisies. She wiped her eyes and cheeks, took a deep breath and answered the questions while the old lady filled in the blanks. When it came to Annie's signature, the lady stopped.

"You'll have to write your name in this spot," she said, pointing to the signature line.

Annie grabbed her throat because it ached again with tears she knew were brewing. Sure enough, they started running down her cheeks and she dabbed them with the pretty hanky. "But I can't," she cried. "I don't know the first thang about words."

The old lady patted her arm and rubbed her back. "Yes, you can," she replied softly. "Look, I'll draw some dots and you just connect them, okay? It'll be fun, like a game."

The old lady had a way about her that didn't make Annie feel stupid, and she breathed easier as she watched the stranger maneuver the pen to make tiny blue circles on the form.

"There," the old lady said when she completed the dots. "Now you take this pen and just follow them."

The pen was clumsy in Annie's hand and she held it like she was about to shovel dirt.

"No, not like that," chuckled the old lady. "Here, place the pen between your thumb and middle finger and rest the tip on the paper. Slowly guide the ball of the pen around the dots. You try it now."

It was awkward at first, but by the time Annie started on her last name, she had the mechanics down to a tee.

"You're doing great!" the old lady cheered.

"So that's my name?" Annie asked, pointing to the signature line.

"Yep, it says 'Annie Barton.' That's right, isn't it?"

"I guess so," said Annie. "I ain't never saw it in words b'fore."

"Now take this clipboard and pen up to that window where that nurse is so they can start taking care of your boy."

Annie walked across the shiny tile floor to the window and gave the nurse the information.

"Thank you," the nurse said, handing the board to the doctor behind her.

About three minutes later, a man entered the waiting room through a connecting door and shouted her name. "Mrs. Barton? Mrs. Annie Barton?" he asked.

She stood up and faced him. "Yes?"

He pointed toward the double doors of the emergency room. "Please walk down the hall to Emergency Room A where your son is. He's waiting for you."

A smile broke out on Annie's puffed red face and she hurriedly walked in the direction that he had pointed. She might not be able to tell what room Emergency Room A was, she thought, but she could sure recognize her own son if she had to peek into every room to find him. But she soon discovered that it wasn't necessary because she saw Will lying on the bed in the very first emergency room.

"Mama?" he mumbled.

Annie beamed. "Yore awake!" she said, walking quickly to his bedside and reaching out for his hand. "Mama was so wurried. But yore such a big boy that I knowed you'd be fine."

She caressed his face and looked at the bump on his little forehead, which wasn't as big as she imagined it to be. It had stopped bleeding, and she pulled his little body toward her for a hug.

"Mama, whar's Dwayne?"

"Now, honey, don't worry 'bout Dwayne. He's with Miss Verneice. Becky, too."

"Whar's Daddy?"

Annie's stomach sickened at the thought of Robert.

"Daddy ain't here, hon. It's just you and me."

Will looked relieved and stared at the blood on his mama's dress. "Mama, yore dress dirty!"

Annie had forgotten all about the dress she was wearing and reached up to feel the smashed daisy in her hair. "Oh, this stupid ol' dress? Don't you fret none, Will. Mama can warsh it out."

She reached over the bed and hugged her son gently. "It's gonna be all right, baby. The doctors will fix you up like brand new."

Annie and Will were unaware that they had company in tiny Emergency Room A. Dr. Jonathan Shea, an emergency doctor from Blytheville, Arkansas, was about to meet his last patient at Herndon General before starting up his own practice in California.

Dr. Shea cleared his throat so he wouldn't startle the young mother and her son.

Annie pulled away from Will's embrace and turned around to face the doctor.

"You must be Mrs. Barton," he said, looking down at her son's chart. "I'm Doctor Shea. I'll be treating little Will."

The doctor reached to shake Annie's hand. She could feel the moistness of his skin, like he had just creamed his hands or something. His sweet cologne smelled up the small room, and the glare from his shining white teeth hypnotized her. She couldn't take her eyes off them the whole time he talked.

"What we're going to do is take Will down to X-ray and take some pictures of his hand," the doctor said.

Annie had no idea that Will's hand had been injured. She looked down at his bruised, pudgy fingers that resembled a catcher's mitt.

"We'll also examine him from head to toe," Dr. Shea said. "But while we're doing that, Mrs. Barton, you'll be more comfortable out in the waiting room. I'll call you when we're done, okay?"

This time Annie looked up beyond his white teeth into his blue eyes that were decorated with long dark lashes that fluttered when he talked. The only ones she had ever seen so big and pretty belonged to her daddy's horse. Dr. Shea was the most handsome man she'd ever seen, and his eyes cast some kind of spell over her, a spell that rendered her unable to hear or speak. All she could do was nod her head.

"One of the nurses might be able to help you clean some of that blood off your arms and dress," he said. "There's a restroom in the waiting room where you can take care of that while we're in X-ray."

The handsome doctor looked at Will and clapped his hands together. "Okay, young man. Are you ready?"

Will nodded, wiping the tears that were trickling down his cheeks.

"Then off we go!" Dr. Shea said. He tugged on Will's gurney, pushing it away from the wall and in the direction of a long hall leading to an X-ray room. Annie stood helpless as her son was wheeled away. She saw Dr. Shea stop to talk to a nurse and then point in Annie's direction. The nurse walked toward her.

"Mrs. Barton, how about I get you a washcloth and show you to the restroom?" asked the nurse, taking Annie's arm and leading her toward the hospital's bathroom.

"Thank you," Annie replied, not knowing exactly what a restroom was, but she was sure it was a good room to be in for mothers who needed a rest.

As they walked, Annie looked at the crumpled handkerchief in her hand that belonged to the old lady in the waiting room. "Oh," she cried, "can we stop in the waiting room furst? I have to give somethang back to a lady."

"Okay," replied the nurse.

When they reached the waiting room, all the seats were filled except Annie's and the old lady's.

"She's not here," said Annie, disappointed.

"Well," said the nurse, "I bet she's either gone home or back in the emergency room area with whomever she came with. The nurse at the window will be able to tell you where she is."

They walked to the window and Annie recognized the nurse who had taken her information. "Ma'am, whar's the ol' lady that set with me over yonder?" she asked, pointing to the chair.

The nurse rose from her seat and looked in the direction of Annie's pointed finger. "I don't remember an old lady ever being in here today," she replied.

"Yes, thar was an ol' lady," said Annie, "and I need to give her hankie back to her. She said her husband had . . . die . . . beet . . . us or somethang like that."

The nurse tried not to laugh. She didn't want to embarrass Annie. "You must mean diabetes, sweetie," she said. "I'll check the admissions list."

Annie was never so sure of anything in her life than she was about the woman who helped her write her name. A sweet old lady like that just doesn't go unnoticed in a room full of babies and young people, she thought.

"No, Mrs. Barton, I have no patient listed with diabetes today or yesterday or the day before. Are you sure you talked to this lady? You were awfully upset when you came in here earlier."

"I'm *very* shore," said Annie sternly. "I know, let me see my paper I wrote."

The nurse came back a few seconds later with Annie's paperwork that she had filled out earlier. *All I have to do is look at the dots 'round my name and that'll show the ol' lady was here. I ain't nuts.*

Annie quickly scanned the page down to the signature line where the nice lady had guided her hand to connect the dots, but she couldn't see any. She squinted her eyes, because sometimes she could see better that way, but there were no dots around her name. 'Annie Barton' was written beautifully in cursive on the last line of the paperwork.

"You have beautiful handwriting," said the emergency room nurse. "Where did you go to school?"

Annie was baffled. Her forehead wrinkled as she looked over at the old lady's empty chair, then at the crumpled handkerchief in her hand and then back at the signature.

"School?" she asked. "School?"

"Yes," the nurse replied. "Where did you go to school?"

Annie hesitated. "Cook," she lied. "I went to school in Cook."

10 / THE ENCOUNTER

"Who'd you carry to Herndon?" Mama D asked Dub as soon as his ambulance pulled up to the preacher's house.

Dub didn't want to tell her it was Annie and Will. He figured she'd find out sooner or later anyway, so he changed the subject quickly. He didn't want to get in the middle of things.

"Is Robert ready to go?" he asked, moving quickly to open the ambulance's doors and get the gurney out.

"Yeah," she replied. "I'll follow you in the truck. Jack's stayin' b'hind."

Dub put Robert on a cot in the back of the ambulance alongside an unconscious Andy Drummond, just in case he woke up suddenly and didn't know where he was. Sheriff Haynes rode shotgun while Dub steered the red emergency vehicle west on the tarred road to Herndon General. The sheriff had to go along to admit the Drummond boy and to make sure the Herndon police had him in their custody during his hospital stay.

Sheriff Haynes had asked Daddy Jack to stay at the jail to watch over Billy, the Drummond boy's partner in crime. But right before Daddy Jack and Ike Burns brought Billy to the jailhouse, they had to release Cornelius Gibbs, whose son, Calvin, had suffered second degree burns from the tar and feathering. There was only one cell in the sheriff's police station, and Cornelius would have killed Billy for sure if they were in the same room.

"Go on home to your family, Cornelius," Daddy Jack said, opening the lock to the black man's cell. "Yore wife and boy need you home."

Cornelius had calmed down considerably from when he was first brought in. It had taken six men to get him into the jail's cell. His veins bulged from his neck and his face was tightened when he found out that Calvin had been harmed. Putting him in the cell was the smart thing to do, considering he was in the frame of mind to kill someone. The only signs of his prior anger now were the cuts on his hands from hitting the jail's brick wall.

Daddy Jack opened the barred doors.

"Yo' done caught dos boys?" Cornelius asked.

Daddy Jack hated to lie, but he knew it was for the best right now.

"Naw," he answered. "But you have my word we will afore mornin', Cornelius."

"I hope dat be true, Mistah Jack," Cornelius said. "Dos mothah fuckahs be playin' wid de chile of de wrong man. I know yo' knowed dat." Then he walked out of the jail toward home. Daddy Jack watched him until he was well out of sight before summoning Ike to bring Billy around to the front door of the jailhouse.

Daddy Jack stared at Cornelius' huge body plowing down the road, his muscular arms and massive hands swinging to and fro like long-handled shovels. For years, Cornelius was known as Cook's "black monster." The name started circulating after Lem Smithers was penned under his automobile back in 1959 when his car's jack slipped. Cornelius happened to be walking by on his way home from the cotton fields when he heard Lem hollering for help. The "black monster," as Lem told it later, reached up under his '55 Chevy and flipped it over off him in just one heave.

But even before the story of Lem and his Chevy had made the rounds of Cook, Cornelius was already being talked about. The first big story about him began circulating twenty years earlier when a wolf wandered onto Cornelius's property, growling and snapping at his children. The tale has varied with each telling as it traveled from mouths to ears and over telephone wires, but the massive strength of Cornelius never changed from tongue to tongue. One variation of the story pitted Cornelius against the beast when he walked out into his yard and saw the wolf creeping toward his baby son, Calvin, who was just three months old then and lying on a blanket in the yard near his older sisters.

Everyone agreed that the old wolf didn't have a prayer any which way you told the story when he met up with the likes of the huge man. Cornelius was said to have reacted without thought, grabbing the animal up by its throat with his bare hands and wringing its neck while the children watched in horror. No, no man wanted to be around Cornelius when he was angry, especially one who'd just tarred and feathered his son.

"C'mon, Ike. Get Billy in here," yelled Daddy Jack. "Cornelius is done out of sight."

*****

Mama D gripped the steering wheel tightly, fearing she'd run off the road or lose sight of the ambulance and get lost. She didn't want to listen to Daddy Jack the rest of her life say, "Women don't know the furst thang 'bout drivin' a car. They b'long in the kitchen, not on the road."

The setting sun shone through her windshield and nearly blinded her. *Whut does that ol' fart know, anyway? I'll show him.*

The emergency entrance to the hospital was crowded, so Mama D parked the truck a short distance away and walked to where the ambulance was backed in. Dub had already taken Robert and Andy inside, and Mama D walked in like she owned the place. She was greeted by an orderly who asked if she needed help.

"I ain't no patient, if that's whut you think," Mama D snapped. "My boy was carried in here. Whar is he?"

"Was he with Mr. Dub?" the orderly asked.

"Yeah, but he's a'walkin'. He's just got a cut arm."

The orderly pointed to the waiting room and told Mama D she needed to fill out paperwork so her son could be treated. Like Annie, Mama D had problems filling out the form. She had dropped out of school before her reading and writing skills were developed, and it frustrated her to have to think so hard. She scribbled what she thought was enough information for the doctors to know, and she did it all from the same seat that Annie had occupied just an hour before.

She returned the clipboard to the nurse at the window and began walking back to her seat when the nurse called her name.

"Excuse me, Mrs. Barton," the nurse said, after glancing at the paperwork. "You're the second Mrs. Barton in here today. Are you related to Annie?"

Mama D whirled around so fast that she almost lost her balance. "Whu'd you say to me?"

"I asked if you were related to Annie Barton. She admitted her son just a little while ago."

"That ain't so," snapped Mama D. "Thar's gotta be a mistik. "Annie's at home with the young-uns."

The nurse scratched her head with the point of her pencil. "Well, would one of them happen to be named Will?"

Mama D snorted. "Annie and Will are here? That can't be right! Whar is she and that boy?"

The nurse, alarmed by Mama D's abrasive reaction, realized that it was not going to be a happy family reunion once she hooked up with Annie, and she had taken such a liking to the young girl.

"Just wait right over there," she said, pointing to the empty chair. "I'll see if she's still here."

The nurse knew exactly where Annie was. She had just taken her down to the restroom to wash up. She left her desk to warn her about the mean-spirited woman in the waiting room.

Annie was standing in the restroom staring at the stalls. She glanced over to the other side of the room and saw three sinks and a huge mirror, and jumped back when she caught sight of herself.

"Good gawd!" she cried. "I'm a'mess!" Blood trickled down both her arms and there were splashes of red all over the front of her yellow dress.

She took the washcloth and ran it under the water to clean her arms, and then spied the toilets behind her in the mirror. She dropped the washcloth in the sink and walked slowly to one of the stalls.

"Well, I'll be," she said, staring at the water inside the toilet. "A real potty, and so clean! Wunder how this thang warshes the doo-doo away?"

She went from stall to stall checking each toilet and there was nothing in any of them. "Gotta be some kinda string to yank or switch somewhere," she decided. As soon as she tugged on the silver lever on the back of one of the toilets, a loud "whoosh" startled her. She looked down and saw the water going down the drain. "So that's it!" she said aloud. "Wunder whar it goes?"

The door to the restroom opened and Annie shut the stall's door. "Mrs. Barton?" asked the nurse. "Mrs. Barton? Are you in here?"

Annie opened the door slowly and stared at the nurse. "I wuz just tryin' to use this thang, that's all," said Annie. "I didn't mean no harm."

"Don't be silly," the nurse laughed. "You can use anything in here. But I must tell you that there's another Mrs. Barton out in the waiting room. Her son is Robert. Is she related to you?"

Annie gasped and held onto the stall's door. Blood drained from her face. "Mama D? Mama D is here? Oh, my gawd, she's madder than a wet hen, right?"

"Well… you could say that," said the nurse. "Is she your kin?"

"Yes, ma'am. I guess she come to take me home."

"Well, I believe she's here because of Robert. He was admitted with an arm wound of some kind," the nurse explained.

Annie's abdomen flinched and she felt vomit rushing up into her throat. She turned around quickly to the toilet and let it go. The nurse handed her the wet washcloth from the sink to wipe her face.

"Did you tell Mama D I wuz in here?" asked Annie, searching the nurse's eyes for some kind of sign that she hadn't.

The nurse sighed. "No, hon, I didn't. Just wash up and I'll keep her in the waiting room. You just go back to your son's bed area and pull the curtains. Stay there until the doctor comes to get you."

The nurse returned to her desk to find an anxious Mama D at her window.

"Whar's the girl?" she asked coldly.

"I couldn't find her," the nurse said nonchalantly. Then she turned away and walked back into the file room.

Mama D knew she was lying. Fuming, she decided to go through the emergency doors on her own to find Annie.

"You can't go in there!" the nurse shouted to Mama D.

But Mama D's heavy torso plunged through the doors like an army tank raiding enemy territory, and she immediately caught sight of Annie's backside. She ran up behind her and slapped the back of her head before Annie had a chance to turn around to see her attacker. The blow forced Annie to the floor.

"Whut in the hell ar' you doin' here, girl?" she screamed. When she raised her hand again to hit Annie – this time across the face – it was caught in mid-air by Dr. Shea. He grabbed her other hand at the wrist.

"Nurse!" he shouted. "Nurse! Get this crazy woman out of here STAT!"

Three nurses and a security guard hauled Mama D out the door into the parking lot. Annie sat on the floor, stunned and embarrassed at her mother-in-law's actions. She was sure Mama D's cursing could be heard on every floor of the hospital.

Dr. Shea reached for Annie's hands and pulled her up onto her feet, and then surprised her by pulling her into his arms.

"It's okay, Mrs. Barton," he said softly, patting her back with one hand and stroking her hair with his other hand. "It's okay. Are you all right?"

Her head rested on his chest against the pocket of his white coat where his nametag was pinned. His sweet cologne was like smelling salts.

She whimpered like a kitten. "It's Annie," she said softly. "Annie."

11 / THE SUCKER

Dub dropped off his passengers and went in search of Annie. As he rounded the corner of the emergency room, he saw her in Dr. Shea's arms.

"Aw, Annie," he said softly, walking toward her and eyeing the doctor. "What a day it's been for you, eh, girl?"

Annie let loose of Dr. Shea's hold and turned to face Dub. "Mr. Dub, can me and my boy hitch a ride back to Cook with you tonight? Providin' that the doctor here says that Will can go, that is."

Dr. Shea looked down at Annie and nodded. "I want to see him in three days, though. I want to make sure he's healing properly. That's a nasty bump on his head. The X-rays haven't come back yet on his hand, but I don't believe it is broken. He can make a fist just fine and I really believe it's just a sprain. I'll let you know when I get the final results. Just keep his arm in a sling until I see him again, and don't let him get too rambunctious."

Annie pretended she knew what an X-ray was and what the word 'rambunctious' meant. She instinctively trusted the doctor, though, and knew that whatever an X-ray was, it was okay if he used it on Will. She reached out to shake his hand.

"Thank you, doctor," she said smiling. "You been nice to me and my boy."

"It was nothing. Just keep his head wound clean and don't let him run around for a day or two. We'll send some bandages home with you, too."

"I've got some in the ambulance if you need more, Mis' Annie," said Dub. "C'mon. Let's go get that little guy."

Will was sitting up in the bed licking a sucker when Dub and Annie walked in. "Look, Mama! Candy!" he said excitedly, holding up the red sucker for her to see.

Annie smiled and tears welled up in her eyes. The nurse, who was standing near Will's bed, walked over to Annie and placed two suckers in her hand. "He said he wanted to take a sucker to his brother and sister. He is just the sweetest thing. You are so lucky."

"Thank you," Annie said, watching her son enjoy his first piece of candy. "Now, c'mon, Will!" she said playfully. "Mr. Dub here is takin' us home! The doctor said yore head is gonna be just fine."

Will sat quietly in his mama's lap all the way home in the front seat of the ambulance. Annie stared straight ahead at the headlights of approaching cars on the highway, flinching in her seat each time they'd pass. She stroked her boy's dark hair and kissed his head. *It don't matter if he ain't Robert's. He's my blood and nobuddy can say he ain't.* Then she thought about Dr. Shea, his sweet smell, and his creamed hands that stroked her hair.

Dreams of a pretty house, a fancy car and sweet words from a gentle man engulfed her thoughts all the way to Cook.

12 / THE PENCIL

Mama D sat outside the emergency exit waiting to hear about Robert's condition. A security guard stood next to her smoking a cigarette. Neither of them said a word to each other. Thirty minutes later the double doors opened and Dr. Shea walked out. She stood up and looked at him like a mad dog with rabies.

"Who you think you are makin' me wait out cheer for my boy? I ain't takin' no more o'yer blather."

Dr. Shea clasped his clipboard and shook his head.

"That girl – why you don't even know whut a problem she is!" she continued. "You had no right to make me leave. That's my kin. Not yorn. You had no right."

The doctor stared at Mama D. He took a deep breath, smiled, and talked slowly. "Mrs. Barton. This is *my* hospital. A hospital where sick people are treated, NOT a hospital where people are slapped around. Your business with your family is your business, but it won't be dealt with in our halls. Consider yourself lucky that you weren't arrested," he said, wiping the sweat from his brow. "Now, about your son."

Mama D was breathing heavy and about to explode. She didn't like being controlled or being told what to do. Everyone in Cook knew her dark side and went out of their way to keep it from hitting the surface. She was just seconds from that happening right there at the emergency exit, but she bit her tongue and shut up.

"Doctor Jones sent me out here to tell you that Robert has a superficial wound and that it should heal just fine. He'd have told you himself, but he was called into emergency surgery. However, Doctor Jones would like to keep him overnight for observation. It would be in your best interest and the interest of your community if you could locate the animal that caused this wound and have it quarantined for ten days."

Pretty fancy words to throw at a countrywoman, she thought. "Whut the hell is quarantined?" she asked, thinking that it sounded like a secret ingredient in Uncle Deek's whiskey.

"It simply means that you need to pen the animal up so it won't get loose for ten days and watch it for any signs of disease, like rabies."

"Rabies? Rabies? Ain't no way in hell my boy's got rabies!"

"Well," Dr. Shea continued, "it's very unlikely. But you'd want to know that for sure, wouldn't you?"

Mama D reluctantly said yes. "It's all that Drummond boy's fault," she snipped. "Stupid, drunk, good-for-nothin' snake. I've a good mind to pen him up with that ol' boar, then shoot the both of them dead."

Dr. Shea rolled his eyes. "I'd advise you not to harm that young man," he warned in a stern voice. "And I'd advise you not to harm your daughter-in-law again. If I see any bruises or cuts on her, I'll have you arrested."

Mama D's mouth fell open.

"Now get out of here and come back tomorrow for your son," he ordered. Then he turned his back on her and walked into his hospital.

****

Two days passed before the old boar was caught. Stinking of whiskey, dried blood and urine, it took three men to run it down and trap it. His squealing body was covered with an oversized tow sack, thrown into the back of a truck, and taken to a pen that Robert and Daddy Jack made behind the barn. Out of sight, but not out of smelling range, the boar reminded Annie of the Barton men in a lot of ways.

Since the hospital encounter, the tension inside the Barton home had grown worse. Robert kept his eyes on the boar like he was a preacher praying for a healing. Mama D was unusually quiet around Annie, but she didn't have to say anything. Her hateful stares were painful enough.

Both Will and Robert were doing fine. Will's eye was bruised, but Dr. Shea told Annie to expect that to happen, and his hand's size was back to normal. Robert's wound appeared to be healing fine, looking more like a bad scrape than a cut from a boar's tooth, but he continued to be doted over by Mama D like a soldier who'd been shot in battle.

Annie decided that she wasn't going to take Will back to Herndon, even though Dr. Shea requested that she bring him back in three days. There was no way the Bartons would let her go anyway, and she didn't trust them to take her boy anywhere. She didn't bother to tell them about the three-day follow-up, even though she would have liked to have seen the handsome doctor again. Dr. Shea was on her mind all the time now. Thinking about him and dreaming of his mouth kissing hers were nice diversions from her daily routine and made life a bit more tolerable.

The day before, just after her creek bath, she spied a pencil on the creek's bank. It reminded her of the pen she used to write her name on the hospital's form, the form that the mysterious little old lady had helped her with. The lady's hankie with the small embroidered daisies was the prettiest thing she'd ever owned, and she hid it under the mattress for fear it would become Mama D's property if found.

Annie sat on the ground with the pencil in her hand and searched for something to write on, like a napkin or a magazine page that usually dotted the bank. Then she remembered the book inside the hollowed log and her excitement grew. Could she remember how to write her name?

She removed the rock and reached for the book. It felt good in her hands, like the Bible her mama took to church. It didn't feel as stiff and hard as she remembered, like maybe the weather had softened it up. The pages showed signs of wear as if they had life in them now. It didn't appear to be just two old pieces of board with stiff papers sandwiched between them.

She turned the pages past the beautiful pictures of table settings, looking for blank pages to write on. The rooster crowed and made her flinch. With each minute, the sun was adding new light to her spot on the creek and she could make out the pages more clearly. The pencil in her hand was a little damp with sweat as she anticipated her new adventure at writing.

"Purdy tables," she said, turning the pages. "Oooh, purdy flowers." She smiled while turning each page, imagining a life surrounded with pretty things. Then she turned to a page that was covered with dots.

"Whut's this?" she said, holding the book up toward the sky's light to get a better look. Squinting, she saw dots similar to the ones the old lady in the hospital had her connect with a pen, the ones that spelled her name. With her heart pounding as loud as Dub's siren, she began connecting them.

The page spelled 'Annie Louise Barton.' Her name! "Annie Louise Barton," she said loudly for the creek animals to hear.

On the next page, the connected dots spelled out another familiar name, one that Annie recognized from a hospital name pin: Dr. Jonathan Shea.

13 / "ROCK OF AGES"

On Wednesday, the third day after Will's accident, Dr. Shea showed up at the Bartons' home.

Annie was in the backyard hanging clothes while all three children napped. Mama D, Daddy Jack, and Robert had left earlier that morning to check out some land they owned down by the cotton gin. Then they were going over to Doc Wilks' to have Robert's arm looked at.

The wild boar was fine and content in the hog-wallow behind the barn. Annie was anxious to finish the wash because she planned to run to the creek and practice some more of her writing before the children awoke. The day after she found Dr. Shea's name in the book, another page appeared with twenty-six different letters that she connected with dots. She was anxious to see what today's page would hold.

No one was in the house except the kids asleep in their beds, and they didn't hear Dr. Shea's knock at the front door. He stood there a good three minutes before deciding to venture to the back of the house. He saw Annie hanging up a sheet and singing. He watched her pin a sheet to the line, and heard lyrics to a song that he knew must have come from her upbringing because she certainly hadn't learned it from the Bartons.

"Rock of ages, land of thee … let me hide myself in thee … Let me walk within yer trees, let me hide myself in thee …"

Dr. Shea couldn't believe his ears. Here was a young woman who had so much love for her children and love of her Lord, yet was imprisoned in a house with evil. How did this happen? What brought her here? He was anxious to know. Never mind that she didn't know the words to the song. It was still beautiful to his ears.

Instead of embarrassing her by interrupting her in mid-song, Dr. Shea walked back to the front of the house and began shouting, "Mrs. Barton?

Mrs. Barton? Are you here, Annie Barton?"

"Back here," shouted Annie. "In the backyard. Who is it?"

She picked up her empty laundry basket and started toward the house when she saw Dr. Shea walking toward her. He was wearing a suit and tie and his dark hair was blowing a little bit in the breeze. He pushed his hair back and smiled widely, showing his beautiful white teeth. Then she smelled his cologne. While floating in the air somehow that cologne sprouted hands and began choking her. She coughed. She could hardly breathe.

"Are you all right?" he asked her.

Annie nodded. "Whut are you doin' here?" she managed to utter.

"How's Will?"

"He's fine."

"Well, when you didn't bring him to Herndon for his checkup, I thought I'd drive over here to see him. I've been wanting to visit Cook for a long time."

"Why?" Annie asked. "Thar's nothin' here in Cook."

That was true, he thought. He was shocked to see most of the homes in poor condition, and he could definitely tell who had good paying jobs and who didn't by the shape of them.

Dr. Shea stumbled for a reply. "Well, I've always heard about Cook, and I've treated a lot of people from Cook, and I just wanted to see what the town looked like, that's all."

"Thar ain't no town," Annie said. "Just a store with a post office inside and a rundown gas station."

Will came to the back door. "Hey!" he shouted at Dr. Shea.

"Well, hey there, yourself, young man!"

Will ran to him and Dr. Shea picked him up. "Say now, that head's looking pretty good. How does the old eye feel?"

"Okay," said Will.

Dr. Shea reached into his coat pocket and pulled out three suckers. "Here's a little something for you and your brother and sister," he said.

"Not Becky," said Will. "She a baby. Can Mama 'ave it?"

"Of course!" he replied.

Dr. Shea put Will down and he ran into the house to give Dwayne the candy.

"I'd ask you inside, but I can't," said Annie. "I can't have no people inside."

"That's okay, Annie," he said. "I need to go anyway. The hospital heard I was coming out here and asked me to check on Doctor Wilks. He's your town doctor, right?"

"Yep."

"Do you know how I can find him?"

"All I knowed is he's got the only blue house in Cook and you can't miss it from the road. Did you see one comin' in?"

"As a matter of fact I did," said Dr. Shea.

"I don't know whut road that is, but that blue house I knowed is his," Annie said. "But be careful. Robert and his maw and paw are goin' thar, too."

"Don't worry your pretty head about them, Annie," he said. "I can take care of them. You take care of yourself, you hear?"

"I will," she said. "Thank you for comin' to see Will."

Dr. Shea paused and then asked, "They aren't hurting you, are they Annie?"

She lowered her eyes. "No."

"You'll let me know if they do, won't you?"

She looked up into his face and smiled. "Yes."

Dr. Shea started to walk toward his car when he remembered why he came to see Annie. "Oh, my goodness, I almost walked away without telling you that the X-rays came back on Will's hand and it was just as we thought. Just a sprain and no broken bones."

Annie smiled. "That's great news, Doctor Shea. Thank you!"

"You're very welcome, my dear, " he replied.

Annie watched him get into his fancy red car and drive off down the road. She could just imagine all the faces in Cook looking out their windows wondering who he was and why he was visiting the Barton home. When Dr. Shea turned left on the road leading out of Cook he saw the blue house.

"Doc Wilks' place," he said, pulling into the driveway.

It looked and sounded like no one was home, but he knocked on the door anyway. No one came right away and he was about to leave when the door opened slowly, revealing the face of an old man Dr. Shea presumed was Doc Wilks.

"Doctor Wilks? Doctor William Wilks?"

"Yeah, who wants to know?"

"Doctor Wilks, I'm Doctor Shea from Herndon General Hospital."

Doc Wilks was baffled. *Was this visit something he had forgotten?* He searched his mind for answers. *What is going on? Why was this man here? Where's Martha? Why isn't she here? She's never here when I need her! Why would someone visit him from the hospital?*

Then Doc Wilks remembered.

"Oh, are you here about Annie?" he asked.

"Annie?" a puzzled Dr. Shea asked. "Annie Barton?"

"Yes," said Dr. Wilks. "Yes, Annie Barton. I guess someone told you about her sterilization. For the life of me, I don't know who that could have been, but I've changed my mind. I'm not going to do it. I don't know what I was thinking."

"Sterilization?"

"Yes," replied Doc Wilks. "C'mon in."

14 / THE CONTRACT

"Don't worry yer purdy li'l head," Annie said to Rusty, like the dog really knew what she was saying.

"Don't worry yer purdy li'l head. Don't you get it, Rusty? Doctor Shea thinks I'm purdy! He thinks I have a purdy head!"

She took off dancing around the backyard with the laundry basket as her partner like Cinderella at the ball. Rusty watched from underneath the house, more interested in chewing on an old bone he had just dug up than listening to the babbling of a lovesick human.

"Don't worry yer purdy li'l head," she said sweetly to the laundry basket as she twirled near the clothesline. "Just don't worry yer purdy li'l head, okay?"

Around and around the yard she danced. Will and Dwayne came out of the house and danced along with her, all of them saying, "Don't worry yer purdy li'l head! Don't worry yer purdy li'l head!" like it was lyrics to a song. Becky was standing in her crib looking out her bedroom window laughing at them and jumping up and down on her mattress.

Annie, Dwayne and Will fell to the ground and rolled over and over laughing and holding their stomachs. The boys didn't know exactly what it was all about. They just knew their mama was happy and that made them happy, too.

They got up from the ground and went inside to get Becky for their planned trip to the creek. This time Annie was not going to allow the boys down near the water. They were just going to play along the bank.

"Get you a stick for the ridey horse," she told Will.

The boys were also eager to swing in the tire that Annie said she would tie from a tree limb. Becky was just anxious to do anything but stay in her crib. And Annie was excited to open her book to see what was new inside to learn.

With the boys taking turns swinging from inside the tire and Becky cooing and reaching for all the birds and squirrels, Annie opened her book. She was now able to write her name without dots. Dr. Shea's, too. She knew all her alphabet letters. Now what was she going to learn? She slowly turned to a new page and was surprised to see pictures of animals and objects with words under them.

She called for the boys. "Dwayne! Will! Come here! Help me with this book."

The boys eagerly helped their mama with the pictures. "That's a hawse, Mama," said Will.

"And that's an ax, Mama," said Dwayne.

"House, H-O-U-S-E," spelled Annie. "Ax, A-X."

Becky clapped her hands.

They spent two hours looking at pictures and spelling objects. "Spider, cow, shoe, fire truck, ambulance, shovel," all words that she knew but had never seen written as words. Annie practiced writing them, too. No dots.

They worked until it was almost suppertime, then they gathered up all their stuff and began their short trek back to the house. Annie had placed the book inside the log and told the boys to keep it a secret. They said they would.

While Annie was preparing the fried chicken, she began thinking about the world outside her house, outside Cook and outside Herndon. She thought about the lady in the long flowing gown dancing with the handsome man.

I wunder whar they live? she thought.

Then she remembered that when she was a little girl, her mama's friend, Betty, moved to California. There was a lot of water there, she knew that much. And sand, too. She decided that the lady in the movie magazine probably lived there.

Mama D, Daddy Jack, and Robert were still not home and it was time. She could tell by the clock's hands. Dinner was always served when the clock's hands were pointing straight up and down.

"It's six o'clock," said Annie, acting like she could tell time.

She heard a car door slam in front of the house and looked out the living room window to see who it was. She knew it wasn't Robert or his parents because they were in the truck and they would have driven up alongside the house. She pulled back the curtains and saw Dr. Shea's car. He was knocking on the front door. Annie ran to open it.

"Doctor Shea! Whut is it?" she asked.

"Annie, we need to talk now," he said, pushing her aside and walking into the living room.

"I thought you went back to Herndon," she said. "Why you still heer?"

He put his hands on her shoulders. "Listen to me carefully, okay?" he asked.

"Okay," she said softly.

"I went to Doc Wilks' place today. Do you remember when I told you that I was going to pay him a visit?"

Annie nodded.

"Well, this Doc Wilks is not mentally stable . . . ah, he is just not right in the head, do you know what I mean?"

Annie nodded her head again. She had heard Mama D say those exact words.

"Anyway, I will say this as plain as I can. Doc Wilks told me that he was going to sterilize you tomorrow. Do you know what that means? He is going to cut on you and make it so you won't have any more children."

"Whuut?"

"And get this: That old bastard who can't even remember one day from the next – shit, more like one minute to the next minute – he was going to actually perform surgery on you in exchange for a piece of property that Robert and his parents own! Are you following me?"

Annie felt like she was in a dream. Wake up! Wake up! Wake up now, Annie, she said to herself.

"Yes, I understand, Doctor Shea," she answered.

"Okay, this is what we're going to do. Listen to me carefully. I drove to Herndon and had my lawyer draw up a document for you. That's a piece of paper that is legal and stands up in a court of law. Do you understand that?"

Annie nodded her head.

"Okay, then. This document says that you understand that certain decisions have been made on your behalf that have not met with your approval. One of those being sterilization. This paper says that you do not authorize any operation by Doctor Wilks or any medical doctor for that matter. It further states that your husband and his parents do not have the right to make decisions for you, that you are of sound mind and body, able to read and write, and physically healthy. Just sign your name on the bottom line, right here."

He pointed to the line and handed her a pen. She grabbed it and signed her name in the most beautiful penmanship he had ever seen. Then

Dr. Shea signed it, too.

"There," he said, picking up the completed document from the table and handing her a copy. "Take this carbon copy and show it to your husband and his parents. They were planning to do this thing tomorrow. I'll come by in the morning to see if you're all right."

Then he grabbed both her shoulders and pulled her toward him, kissing her forehead.

"God, Annie," he whispered into her face. "Can you believe they were going to do this to you?"

Annie was numb. *Anybuddy kin do anythang to me right now.*
This is just a dream.

15 / THE STAND

"I never in my life seen anythang like this," Mama D said as she watched Daddy Jack and Robert try to get the truck out of the mud. "Y'all been stuck thar for three hours. I say it's time to start walkin'. We can call Dub from Deek's place to bring his wrecker."

"Yer right, Maw," said Robert. "C'mon, Daddy."

Daddy Jack wasn't happy about calling a wrecker. Dub charged five dollars and that was five dollars he could spend at Deek's. But he gave in because he was hungry and he knew Annie would have supper ready.

"Doc can look at'cha arm t'mara, okay, son?" said Mama D to Robert.

"Okay, Maw."

Deek was happy to see the three Bartons walking up the road. Daddy Jack was one of his best customers. He let them use his phone to call Dub, and then offered them a drink.

"Want a chaw o'terbacker, Jack?" Deek asked.

Mama D's eyes squinted at her husband. He took a plug anyway. She was already mad at him for getting the truck stuck in the mud. If he hadn't decided at the last minute to check on some land he was having Cornelius clear, they'd have already been to Doc's and be at home eating supper.

Dub pulled up in ten minutes and they all had another drink with him before taking off in the wrecker to get the truck out of the mud. The Bartons walked in the front door of their home at six-thirty. Daddy Jack could smell the fried chicken from the driveway.

"Girl!" Mama D shouted. "Girl! Fetch us some vittles, girl!"

Annie did not respond.

"Girl! Whar the hell are you?"

"I'm right here, Mama D," Annie said. "Whut do you want?"

"Whut do I want? Whut do I want? Is that ah way you tawk to me? *Whut do I want? WE* want our food. Now go fetch it!" she screamed.

Annie stood firm on her two feet with her arms crossed, trying to act like Verneice on the day she saw her stand up to Mama D.

"B'fore I go *fetch* anythang, Mama D, thar is somethang we need to tawk about."

"Oh, thar is, Miz Biggety," said Mama D, folding her arms across her chest. "And just whut would that be?"

"Sterilization," Annie said.

Mama D was dumbfounded. She didn't think Annie could even say the word. "Daddy! Robert! Get in here!" she screamed.

They both ran into the living room.

"Sterilization," Annie said again. "Y'all were gonna do that to me t'mara?"
Robert stumbled for words. "Well . . . Annie . . . yeah, we was . . ."
Frustrated with Robert's response, Mama D lashed out at him. "Whut have I raised? A big fat pussy, that's whut! Dad-burned it, Robert, tell her she ain't got no say! She'll do as we say."
Robert toughened up. "Yeah, Annie. You don't have no say. Doc Wilks already said he'd do it. We can't have no more young-uns. It's the only way."

Annie calmly reached into her apron's pocket, pulled out the carbon copy of the legal document and handed it to her husband.

"No, Robert, yore wrong. I *do* have a say."

"Whut's this?" he said as he unfolded the paper. His mouthed dropped as his eyes scanned the printed material and Annie's signature. He handed it to Mama D. Her mouth fell open, too. Daddy Jack put on his glasses and read it next.

"'This writin' ain't yores,'" Daddy Jack said. "You cain't write."

Annie pulled a pencil from the other pocket of her apron and grabbed the papers out of Daddy Jack's hands. She placed them on the coffee table and wrote her full name, as pretty as you please on the back of the legal document.

The Bartons watched in disbelief. For the first time in many years, Mama D was speechless.

"Supper's ready," said Annie, walking toward the kitchen.

They all sat down to a beautifully decorated table with flowers, placemats, lots of silverware, fried chicken, mashed potatoes, gravy, fried okra, buttered cornbread and iced tea.

And no one said a word.

16 / THE PIE

Annie was bathing the boys in an old washtub on the back porch when she heard the front door slam. She quickly pulled each one from the water, dried them off and sent them to their room to put on their underwear and t-shirts and go to bed. It was late, *too* late for company. Something must be wrong. Maybe it was the sheriff coming to arrest the Bartons for what they were going to have Doc Wilks do to her, she thought. Or maybe it was Dr. Shea coming back to see if everything was okay.

Everything *was* okay. At least for now. Earlier that evening, the Bartons finished their supper without a noise, except for the usual smacking and belching. All three had fallen asleep in the living room when the knock came. Annie was anxious to see who it was and what they were saying. She crept into the dark kitchen within earshot of the living room.

"Why, Mrs. Gibbs, c'mon in," Daddy Jack said, half awake, probably thinking he was dreaming about this large Negro woman standing inside his door. "Whut brung you out this late at night?"

Ethelyn Gibbs knew she was taking a risk visiting the home of white folks late at night, especially going to their front door. She was nervous, staring at the floor and stumbling for words.

"This'n fo' yo' boy, Mistah B," she said, handing him a plate that was covered with a dishcloth. "I heered whut he do fo' my baby, and dis heer ain't much, but I does thank him."

Mama D got up from the couch and grabbed the plate from Daddy Jack's hands. "Mmmmmmmm. This ain't yer famous bluebarry pie, is it, Ethelyn?" she asked.

"H'it shore is, ma'am. How yer boy doin'?"

Robert rose from the chair and yawned, "I'm a sight better, Ethelyn.

That ol' boar just nick't me some, that's all. See?" he said, rolling up his sleeve and pointing to his wound. "Just ah scratch."

Ethelyn took a small step toward Robert and squinted her eyes to see clearly. The sore appeared to be puffed and swollen, not a scratch at all. Her face wrinkled.

"Lawd, Mistah Robert," she said softly. "It done took a turn fo' de wurst, I do declare, cuz it don't look like no scratch at'tall. It got poizon inside, I thinks."

Robert went over to the lamp for a closer look. "It's all swoll up, Maw!"

"Let me look at that, boy!" said Mama D, yanking at his arm. "Oh, that ain't nothin'," she said. "It's just festered some, but ain't *that* bad. Ain't nothin' that a li'l alcohol won't fix. Go on in yonder and have that girl put some on it," she ordered.

Ethelyn wasn't about to tell Mama D any different. Black folk didn't tell white folk what to do. Not in Cook, anyhow.

"How yer boy, Ethelyn?" Daddy Jack asked.

Ethelyn smiled, showing a mouth of missing teeth. "Oh, he jis fine, Mistah B. He jis fine."

"Good. Good," Daddy Jack replied. "We wuz worried about him. That ol' tar can really burn bad. But Larry, I mean Sheriff Haynes, said that them boys didn't smear much on Calvin, only enuff to stick the feathers, an' that it waddn't too hot."

Ethelyn reached for the doorknob. "Well, I'z better be a'steppin' now," she said. "I jis wanna thank y'all fo' helpin' catch dim bad boys dat tarred my Cal. I hope yous likes de pie."

"Oh, we will," said Mama D. "Here. Take this cloth a'back. We'll get yer bowl back to you, too."

"Naw," said Ethelyn. "Y'all jis keeps it."

After the door closed, Mama D went into the kitchen to put the pie down and check on Robert. Annie was swabbing alcohol on his arm.

"Maw," Robert said. "This don't look good. Maybe we ought'ta go back to the hospital and get it check't. My stummick's all tore up, like I gotta throw up."

Mama D waved him off and pulled out the silverware drawer looking for something to cut the pie with. "Why, if that Ethelyn waddn't colored, she'd be rich from folks all over the state wantin' to buy her pies," she said, scooping a huge slice with a spoon and putting it in her mouth. "Mmmmmmmmm," she said. "Mmmmmmmmmmmmm."

Annie didn't give a hoot about Robert, but she was concerned about the sore, too. The old boar was still kicking outside in the pen, smelling up the place like a polecat, and wasn't showing any signs of being sick with rabies. But Robert's wound was getting worse instead of better. She blamed him for not keeping it clean, for stinking himself all the time.

He deserves this, she thought, wiping the puffed red flesh. *He deserves this*.

17 / THE FORK

"Somethang's different," said Annie when she walked to the creek for her morning bath. "Somethang's *really* different."

She looked around for any signs of change, anything out of the ordinary that she hadn't seen before. Nothing. The rooster crowed on time. The birds were nestling in the trees. A slight breeze swayed the branches and leaves, and the water was cool and refreshing.

But Annie still had a nagging feeling that something was different. As she floated in the water daydreaming about Dr. Shea, she heard the screen door slam.

"Robert," she thought, rolling her eyes. "That must be Robert goin' for a pee."

He had tossed and turned all night and Annie barely got a wink of sleep. He'd roll over on his bad arm and let out a whimper, then roll over onto his good arm. Then he'd lie on his back and snore and wake himself up, only to roll over again on his bad arm and whimper. That went on all night.

"Too bad it's not his pee-pee that's got the sore," said Annie aloud. "That would teach him. He deserves that."

She realized what that "somethang different" was as soon as those words left her mouth.

"Oh, my stars!" she squealed. "Oh, my beautiful stars in Heaven! It's *me*! It's *me* that's different!"

For years she had been afraid of Robert waking up and finding her gone in the morning, which would have put an end to her creek bathing and no telling what else. Maybe he'd slap her around some or a lot, she thought. Or tell Mama D and Daddy Jack, and then they'd slap her around, too. Maybe he'd even tell Daddy Jack it was okay to get back on top of her.

But this morning she had no fear of Robert or Mama D or Daddy Jack. "Who cares if they find out I'm in the creek? Who cares if they tell me I can't do it no more? Whut are they gonna do? Chain me to the bed? Whut harm is a bath? If the Bartons bathed more they wouldn't be so sick all the time and Robert wouldn't have that stinkin' sore."

Her newfound strength was a glorious feeling. "No ones gonna hurt me anymore. No one."

She finished her bath and wiped herself dry without even looking back at the house to see if a light was on. *She didn't care.* Snuggled in her robe, she sat on the creek's bank and opened her book. She could hardly wait to see what new surprise the book had for her this morning. She opened it to her bookmark, a thin piece of tree bark she'd found on the bank, and saw a shape she'd never seen before. She spelled out the word underneath it: T-E-N-N-E-S-S-E-E.

On the next page, there were a whole bunch of shapes touching each other. "T-H-E U-N-I-T-E-D S-T-A-T-E-S." She saw California and smiled. "Well, I'll be! Here is California!" She ran her fingers down the state's outline. "It sure is funny lookin'!"

She spelled all the states and tried to pronounce each name, then decided she'd better get back to the house. She couldn't wait to get the kids all to herself to share the book's new lesson. Becky was standing up in her crib looking out the window as Annie approached the back of the house. Annie waved to her. Becky jumped up and down, laughing.

"Good morning, baby girl!" Annie said to Becky. "Isn't it a beautiful day?"

Becky clapped her hands. The boys were rustling in their bed. "C'mon, little guys, get up!" said Annie to the boys. "Let's get brekfust over with. I've got a big surprise for you later."

Annie changed Becky's diaper and put her to her breast. The boys reluctantly got up and sat at the kitchen table. With her free hand, Annie poured them some cold cereal and milk.

"Whut's the surprise, Mama?" Dwayne asked.

"Shhhhhhhh," Annie said, putting her index finger to her mouth. "If you say it too loud, it won't be a surprise, will it?"

Dwayne nodded.

"Doctor Shea is comin' here today, Will," she said to her youngest boy.

Will looked puzzled, but happy. "Why, Mama?" he asked.

"Oh, just to say 'howdy' I guess," she answered. "He likes us, you know."

"And he thinks you have a purdy head, too, Mama," Dwayne laughed.

"Yeah," Will said. "You got a purdy head, Mama."

Both boys spit up a little of their milk while laughing.

"Now you boys stop that!" Annie said, playfully.

Robert entered the doorway. "Whut in Sam Hill is going on in here?" he shouted. "Can't a man get any dadgum sleep?"

The boys quieted. Annie poured Robert a cup of coffee and then started frying bacon. He sat down at the table and stared at them. The boys had their heads down so low they almost dipped their hair in their cereal.

Robert winced with pain and grabbed his arm. "Gall darn, blasted arm," he said. "Kept me up all night. Gotta be somethang bad wrong with it."

Annie turned the bacon.

"Did you hear me, Annie?" he said louder. "Gotta be something bad awful."

She just looked at him and turned back to the stove.

Robert stood up fast and pushed the chair back with his legs. He took a step toward Annie with his good arm up in the air like he was going to wallop her a good one.

Annie swung around with her arm up over her head. The fork in her hand was in a striking position, like she was about to stab him. A frightened Becky bit down on her nipple and Annie screamed, "Don't you touch me, Robert Barton, or I'll give you *two* bad arms to cry about!"

Robert slowly dropped his arm. His face was red and his rotten breath hit her face. He stood there looking at her, not believing what he was seeing and hearing.

"Who the hell you think you are?" he shouted. "You ain't nothin', and I'll tell you how nothin', okay? Look at me, girl, right now!"

Annie glared at him, her fork still held high, her lip quivering.

"Yore daddy stole three bags of pecans from my daddy's land and wuz goin' to jail if he didn't pay up. He give you to us for payment."

The words hit Annie like an iron skillet to the head. She lowered the fork. Her body felt weak, like it wanted to fall down and stop breathing. Her eyes filled with tears and she wiped them with her apron. She didn't know about the trade. How could she be so happy with herself one minute and the next minute want to die? And then something came over her, a strong force within; a fighting force she knew she had but never let show. *Ain't nobody gonna talk to me like I'm nothin'. Ain't nobody gonna say I'm not worth nothin'.*

"Whut in tarnation is goin' on in that kitchen?" Mama D shouted from the bedroom. "Y'all better keep that rumpus down or thar'll be hell to pay, ya' hear?"

Robert walked over to the pee closet off the kitchen and Annie turned around to retrieve the bacon from the grease. He came back a few minutes later and she had a plate ready for him to eat.

"You'll pay for this, girl," he said, as he chewed a piece of bacon. "You'll pay bad for this."

PIG DOG CREEK

Annie acted like she wasn't hearing a word he was saying. She walked into the bedroom and put Becky in her crib. Then she shooed the boys from the table and into their room to get dressed. She threw on a cotton dress and ran a comb through her clean hair. When she returned to the kitchen, Robert was gone. His half-eaten plate of food was on the table. She looked out the living room window and saw him walking down the dirt road holding his arm. Mama D shouted to him from her bedroom window.

"Whar you goin', boy?"

Robert stopped and turned around. "To see Doc Wilks, Maw. My arm's ah'killin' me."

Annie returned to the kitchen and began fixing breakfast for Mama D and Daddy Jack. They were just about finished when a car pulled up in front of the house. Mama D ran to the window.

"It's that damned doctor from Herndon," she said. "Whut in the hell is he doin' here?"

Annie ran her fingers through her hair and smiled.

18 / THE GOODBYE

Martha Wilks was in her kitchen stirring oatmeal on the stove when Robert banged on her front door.

"Doc!" he shouted. "Doc! I gotta see you, Doc!"

Martha put down the spoon, wiped her hands on her apron, hurried to the door and opened it. "Why, Robert," she said. "What on earth is the matter?"

"It's my arm," Mis' Martha. "It's real bad."

Martha looked at the swollen arm. "Well, well . . . ," she sighed, gazing at the infected sore. "Well, well," she said again. "You've certainly got an infected sore, that's for sure, but I don't know what William can do for you."

Robert sensed he was about to faint and braced himself on the door's frame. "Whut do you mean, Mis' Martha? He's got to have somethang I can take for this pain."

Martha could see that the young man was hurting, so she motioned for him to come into the house and sit down. "Can I get you anything, son?" she asked. "A glass of water, perhaps? Iced tea . . . "

"No, damn it!" he snapped. "Jest git me the doc!"

Martha was startled by his tone. "I'm afraid that's impossible, dear. He's had another one of his spells, and this time I don't think he's going to snap out of it."

Robert put his head in his good hand and combed back his greasy hair with his fingers. Trembling with pain and frustration he replied, "Is he here?"

"Yes, he's here, dear. He just doesn't know where he is, who I am or who he is, either. Come. Come see for yourself."

She led Robert into the bedroom to Doc Wilks. He was under the blankets with just his eyes peeking out from under the covers. He watched the two of them enter his room, his eyes following their every move.

"He's been like this since yesterday afternoon," explained Martha. "He doesn't talk. He doesn't move. I have to force food and water down his throat. He's really in bad shape."

Robert stood staring at him. He sat down on the edge of the bed and tried to get him to talk. "Doc, it's me, Robert. Robert Barton. I need yer help."

Robert pointed to the sore on his arm and he saw Doc's eyes grow larger. "Yeah, Doc. You recognize this, huh? It's where that damn ol' boar nick't me, 'member?"

Doc breathed harder and fidgeted in his bed. Then he started to moan louder and louder.

"Move away from him, Robert," ordered Martha. "You've got him all upset now."

She stroked Doc's forehead and patted his shoulders to get him to calm down. "He's not any good to you, son. Please let him be. You'll have to get help somewhere else. Now, please leave us."

Robert turned to leave the room and he could hear Martha whispering soothing words to her husband, which seemed to ease Doc's moaning. He left their house and began walking toward home, knowing that his only alternative now would be a doctor at Herndon General Hospital.

While walking back down the road, he saw a red fancy car parked in front of his house and a man standing at the door. He accelerated his pace when he heard his maw screaming at the person through the screen door.

"Git out! Git the hell out!" Mama D shouted at Dr. Shea. "Git off my property and do it now!"

Dr. Shea stood there calmly and let Mama D vent. He tried to get a word in every time she took a deep breath between sentences, but the calloused woman was skilled at throwing out a good tongue-lashing. Through the screen, he could see Annie's blonde hair and blue eyes peeking around the corner from the kitchen, watching and listening to her loony mother-in-law and staring at him with anxious eyes.

Robert sneaked up the steps behind him and swung Dr. Shea around to meet him eye-to-eye. Their noses almost touched, and Dr. Shea's nose wrinkled up from Robert's smell like he had just tasted something sour.

"Whut's goin' on here, Mister? Whut the hell do you want?" he yelled at the doctor, who was covering his nose.

"It's that slick-faced doctor from Herndon," Mama D yelled out. "The one who took up for Annie. The one who was mean to me. Kicked me out of the hospital, that's whut he done."

Robert's left eyebrow rose at the sound of the word 'doctor' and a slight smirk appeared on his face.

"Oh," said Robert, dusting off Dr. Shea's suit coat lapel. "Don't pay my maw no mind. She gits all fussed up when strangers come knockin'. Come on in."

Mama D stood at the door with her mouth agape. "Why, I never seen the likes of . . ."

Robert cut her off in mid-sentence. "Now, Maw, I know whut yer thinkin,' but trust me. It's okay," he said, as he steered Dr. Shea past her into the living room.

"I don't want to cause any trouble, Mrs. Barton," Dr. Shea said, holding up both his hands like he was surrendering to the bad guys.

"Well, then, what brung ye up here this way-off?" she asked.

Dr. Shea paused for a moment before answering. He knew that what he was about to say would have an effect on Annie, and he knew she was listening to their conversation from the other room. He had grown fond of her, and even thought about her in a romantic way when he was alone at night. He could sense that she, too, was developing feelings for him. But there was no future for them. She was married, and he was on his way out west.

"I just want to check on Will's head, that's all," he said.

But what Dr. Shea *really* wanted was to see if Annie was still alive after showing the Bartons the legal papers the night before. He also had something to tell Annie that he had hoped to tell her the day before, but he couldn't quite get the words out. So he decided just to blurt it out now.

"I'm leaving Herndon General in a few days and I'd just like to see Will one more time," he said nervously.

Annie felt like someone had just taken the biggest butcher knife in the kitchen drawer and stabbed it right into her gut. *Leaving? Leaving the hospital? I'll never see him again!*

"Annie!" Robert hollered. "Annie! Fetch Will for the doc."

Annie wiped away the tears that trickled down her cheeks and walked to the back porch to get Will. He and Dwayne were playing with some small rusted cars they'd found along the creek's bank. She hated to disturb him and bring him into the living room with Mama D acting like such a fool, but it was her last chance to come face-to-face with Dr. Shea. She hoped she could stop crying.

Annie led Will by the hand into the living room where Dr. Shea was sitting. "Hello there, young man!" said Dr. Shea. He looked up at Annie. Their eyes met briefly, before Annie lowered hers to the ground.

"Hello, Mrs. Barton."

Annie nodded.

An excited Will ran into his arms. "You got suckers a'gin?" asked Will.

Dr. Shea reached into his pocket. "Here's one for you and one for your brother," he said, handing the suckers to the toddler. "How's that head doing?"

"It's jest fine, doctor," Annie said softly, her lips trembling.

"Well, I just wanted to see him before I left for California," he said. "I'm leaving in a few days to set up a practice out there."

Annie didn't reply. She gazed at Dr. Shea like she was in a trance. Then Robert spoke up.

"Well, doc, since yer here, take a look at my arm, will ya?" he asked.

Dr. Shea put Will down and turned toward Robert. "Ah, the boar wound, right? I thought that had healed."

Robert refreshed his memory about the incident with the boar, how they'd quarantined the animal and how the sore got better, then turned worse. Dr. Shea didn't look happy when he saw it.

"Well, Mr. Barton, I'd say you've got a major infection in this wound, one that would require some thorough cleaning and an antibiotic. If I were you, I'd get it taken care of as soon as possible, like *today*."

That wasn't what Robert wanted to hear. He wanted the doctor to fix it right then and there.

"Can't you give me some easin' powder, doc?" Robert asked.

"I don't have anything like that with me. Come to the hospital later. I go on duty at three."

Robert said he'd be there, and then the doctor said his goodbyes. Annie gathered up her three kids and went to the backyard. Becky sat on a blanket while the two boys played ball with the dog. She weeded the garden, dripping tears on the collard greens and turnips.

"Nuthin' gits nuthin'," she said over and over, yanking at the weeds like they were feathers on a dead chicken. "Nuthin' gits nuthin' and I'm nuthin'."

19 / THE NEWS

By the time the Bartons reached Herndon General Hospital for the three o'clock appointment with Dr. Shea, Robert had a fever of 104 degrees and could barely walk. Dr. Shea immediately called for blood to be drawn to analyze. The nurses in the emergency room scurried around to comply with the doctor's orders to prepare the wound for possible surgery.

Mama D and Daddy Jack found two chairs in the waiting room and sat down. The two nurses on duty behind the glass window were staring at Mama D and whispering to each other.

"Well if that don't beat all," said the older nurse to the younger one. "That's that old bag that slapped her daughter-in-law in the emergency room, remember? That cute little blonde girl that brought her son in with a head wound?"

The young nurse thought a minute. "Yeah, I remember. And Doctor Shea kicked her out. The security guard said she was saying nasty things about Doctor Shea while she was standing outside with him."

The older nurse shook her head side to side. "I can't believe Doctor Shea agreed to treat that old bag's son after all that," she replied. "Better keep an eye on those two. We could have trouble if things don't go their way."

Mama D turned her head toward the two gossiping nurses and they both stared back. "What a nightmare it must be to live with that woman!" said the older nurse, sorting through some files. "Wonder how that sweet young girl is doing?"

Annie wasn't doing well at all. She sat on the steps of the back porch and stared into space while her two boys played in the yard. With tears trickling down her cheeks, she thought about Dr. Shea's last words.

California. He's moving to California. I'll never see him again.

Her stomach ached like she'd eaten something rotten. A sharp pain shot through her abdomen and she ran to the outhouse to get rid of the poison. When she came out, the boys were sitting on the ground outside the door waiting for her.

"Are you okay, Mama?" asked Dwayne.

Annie wiped her wet eyes with her hands. "Yes," she said, sniffing.

Dwayne looked confused. "Are you wurried 'bout Daddy's arm?" he asked.

"Daddy's arm?" she asked. *Daddy's arm?* She hadn't even thought about Robert's arm! She wasn't about to let the children think she was worried about their daddy!

Annie bent down and ran her hand through Dwayne's hair and kissed his forehead. "Why, no, pumpkin," she replied. "Mama jest had a little tummy ache, that's all. Now, let's go inside and see whut we can fix for supper, okay?"

Dwayne nodded and grabbed her hand. Will grabbed the other hand and the three of them walked toward the house. Becky was watching them from the bedroom window.

"Why looky thar," said Annie, pointing to the window. "Miss Becky is up."

Becky smiled a big one-toothed grin and began clapping her hands together. As she did, she lost her grip on the crib's railing and fell backwards out of sight. All three of them laughed and ran up the porch's steps and into the house. Annie shushed the boys, holding them back and peering around the bedroom door. "Whar's our Becky girl, boys?" she asked, looking around the room as if Becky wasn't there. "One minute she's here, and then poof! She's gone."

Becky was lying on her back looking through the crib's slats. Dwayne and Will were holding their mouths to keep from laughing out loud. Annie pretended she didn't see Becky. She picked up a blanket on the floor and said, "Becky, are you under thar?" She looked back at the boys and said,

"No, she ain't here."

Then she moved over to the closet door. "I know yer in thar, Becky girl." She opened the door quickly and the boys let out a muffled squeal. "No, no, Becky girl isn't here. I wonder whar she could be, boys."

Just then Becky stood up in her bed. She unfurled her fingers from the crib's railing and extended her arms to her mama. A huge smile broke out on her face. "Why, thar she is!" Annie yelled. "Thar's my baby girl! Look boys! Look who I found!"

Annie picked up Becky and hugged her tightly. She felt so wonderful in Annie's arms. The boys were giggling like crazy, rolling over and over on top of each other and getting tangled up in the bed's covers. While Annie was changing the baby, she looked out the window and saw Dub walking around the house toward the back door.

"C'mon, boys," she said. "We got company." All four of them greeted Dub at the door.

"Howdy, Mis' Annie," said Dub, touching the rim of his baseball cap.

"Well, howdy yerself, Mr. Dub," Annie replied.

"I knocked on your front door but there was no answer," he said. "I knew you was here somewheres."

"How can I help you, Mr. Dub?" she asked nicely.

Dub took off his ball cap and scratched his head. "I have some news for you from Herndon about your kinfolk. Can I come in and sit a spell?"

Annie hesitated. She wasn't allowed to let anyone in the house when she was home alone, but Dub wasn't just anyone. He was a friend of the family and she trusted him, so she opened the door wider for him to enter.

"Thank you, ma'am," he said, grabbing a chair from the around the kitchen table.

"Would you like a cup of coffee, Mr. Dub?" she asked.

"Naw," he replied. "I can't stay long. Just wanted to let y'all know that Jack . . . *ahem* . . . yore Daddy Jack . . . called me from the hospital in Herndon and they won't be coming home tonight."

Annie fought back a smile. "Whut?" she asked.

"Well," Dub continued, "it seems that Robert is in pretty bad shape and they are gonna stay in Herndon tonight instead of coming home. They're staying at Helen's. He said he'll call me t'mara and let me know more."

Annie stared at him with a blank look. Becky was clawing at her breast. Dub could see that it was time to go, but he was concerned that Annie was afraid to be alone.

"Are you going to be all right for the night, Mis' Annie?" he asked.

Annie managed a faint smile. "Yes," she replied. "We'll be jest fine. Thank you, Dub. Thank you for coming over to tell us."

Dub got up to leave. There was something about Annie that he couldn't quite figure out. He looked her over from head to toe.

"Whut, Dub?" she asked.

"Nothin,' I just want you to know that if there's anything you need, you just go over to Verneice's and use the phone to call me, okay?"

"Okay," Annie replied. "Don't worry. We'll be fine."

Annie closed the door behind Dub and tried to hold back a burst of laughter until he was out of ear range.

"Yipppeeeee!" she shouted to the kids. "Can you believe it, boys? They ain't comin' home. Quick! Pinch me, Dwayne. Pinch me cuz I gotta be dreamin.'"

Dwayne ran over to his mom and pinched her arm softly. Annie pretended to feel the prick of his fingers.

"Ouch! That hurts!" she shouted. "Nope, I ain't dreamin.' I'm wide awake."

She looked around the house and didn't know what to do first. Then she spied the television set.

In a voice that sounded a little bit full of herself, Annie said, "Boys, let's go sit a spell in the living room and watch a little TV."

Dwayne and Will looked at each other and burst into laughter. They ran to the living room and begin fiddling with the knobs.

"Wait now," instructed Annie. "I think you turn it on first."

She remembered seeing Mama D turn the left knob first so she moved it to the right. "Now wait for just a minute," she told the boys. "It'll come on. Then we move this knob here." She pointed to the channel changer.

The boys sat on the floor in front of the set and waited. Slowly, an image appeared. Annie moved the channel changer back and forth and realized there were only three to choose from. The boys chose to watch the one with a little boy and his dog.

Annie nursed and rocked the baby while the boys sat glued to the set. She enjoyed the television, mostly the short little scenes between the shows, like the one where the little boy with the funny hat drops pills into a glass of water and sings '*Plop plop, fizz fizz. Oh! What a relief it is.*'

"He is just the cutest little thang, isn't he boys?" Annie asked.

Dwayne and Will tried to remember the words so they could sing the song later, but they were a little confused.

"Whut does *plop* mean, Mama?" Dwayne asked.

Annie shrugged her shoulders.

After Annie put Becky down for the night, she fixed a late supper for her and the boys. She let them eat the white beans and cornbread in front of the television set only if they promised to be careful.

Hours passed and the boys conked out in front of the set. Annie picked them up one by one and carried them to their bed. She returned to the living room and watched the television until it ran out of shows. She knew it was done for the day because the picture of the Indian chief inside a dartboard was all that was left on the screen. That, and a horrible buzzing sound that hurt her ears.

She turned the TV off and wiped it down with a cloth. It was late — the latest she'd ever stayed up in her life, she was sure of that. She double-checked the doors and windows throughout the entire house to make sure they were locked, and then got ready for bed. As she sat on the bed and brushed her hair, she thought of how wonderful it was to do whatever she wanted with her children and not have to listen to Mama D, Daddy Jack or Robert yelling at her or arguing amongst themselves.

I hope they never come home.

Never, ever.

20 / FREEDOM

Annie and the kids slept late. Will, the first one up, was a little confused because he was *never* first. He wandered into his mother's room and found her sound asleep. He shook her arm gently. A startled Annie opened her eyes and looked into Will's chubby little face.

"C'mon, Mama. Git up," he begged.

Annie shot up in the bed. "What's wrong?" she asked loudly, looking around the room. "Whar's Becky? I mean, *where's* Dwayne?"

"Sleepin,'" said Will calmly. "C'mon, Mama."

He tugged on Annie's arm and she stumbled out of bed. Becky was standing in the crib looking at them and she picked up the baby and walked down the hall. Dwayne was waking up and stretching in his bed. He smiled when he saw her.

The house was quiet and peaceful. Now fully awake, Annie remembered that they were alone in the house. She changed Becky's diaper and placed her in the bed with Dwayne. Then she scooped up Will and got in the bed, too, and the four of them talked about what they were going to do that day.

"I say we go down to the creek right after breakfast," said Annie, holding Becky up in the air above the boys. "We'll take a blanket and some snacks to have later. Okay?"

"Okay, Mama," said Will. "Kin we swing?"

"Yes, you *can* swing on the tire. You *can* even get wet in the crick. I mean *creek*," she said. Then she added sternly, "But no falling on your *head*, okay?"

"Okay, Mama," he said.

"Kin we read from the book, too?" Dwayne asked.

"Of course," replied Annie, wondering what new things they would learn from the book today. "We *can* do *anything* we want to do *anytime* we want to do it."

*****

The month of June is nearing, Annie thought, while stepping out from the back porch onto the grass to hang a load of laundry before going to the creek. The clouds were thinner and the sky seemed a bit bluer, and there were sounds of insects in the trees that Annie knew were associated with warmer weather and crop harvesting.

She put the basket with the wet clothes on the ground and pulled out a sheet to hang first, but she had forgotten the bag of clothespins that were still hanging on a nail on the back porch. As she walked back toward the house, she heard Verneice's screen door slam two houses away, and then she heard her high-pitched voice that silenced the birds and insects above her in the tree.

"Yoo-hoo, shuggar," yelled Verneice, her arm waving high in the air to summon Annie. "Hold on thar a minute."

Annie smiled and waved back at the funny little lady that she thought was the bravest woman to ever walk the earth, besides her own mama, of course. She walked over to the rickety chain-link fence that surrounded the Barton property and met her face-to-face. Annie caught a whiff of Verneice's perfume emanating from what she figured was a freshly bathed body clothed in a clean, flowered muumuu, accented with dangling shell earrings. Her hair was piled high in curls atop her head. Her shiny red toenails, visible in her cutout shoes, matched her red lipstick.

"Hey, girl!" Verneice said. "You're not gonna believe who called me this morning!"

Annie's forehead wrinkled.

"Why, your very own Mama D!" Verneice answered. "Can you believe that old biddy called me? I like to died! And she was as sweet as punch. She told me to tell you that Robert's taken a turn for the worst and that she and Daddy Jack wouldn't be home for a day or two. I guess she'd tried to call Dub but couldn't reach him, so she called me. Can you honestly believe it?"

Annie's head slumped, trying to absorb what Verneice was saying.

"Why, little girl, you look so sad. I thought you'd be happy with that kinda news!"

Annie wasn't sad. It was good news, all right. But the food was low and she had hoped they'd at least come home over the weekend to bring her some and then go back to Mama D's sister's in Herndon. But they really didn't care about her, she knew that. Thinking about her and the kids and their welfare was the furthest thing from their minds. So why did she even call in the first place? Annie asked Verneice.

"Well, it seems she wants you to do something," said Verneice.

Annie crossed her arms. "Like what?"

"Mama D wants you to tell Dub to bring his trailer 'round next time and take the hogs to his place until they get back. And she said for me to tell you to make sure you check those chickens every day for eggs."

"That's it?" asked Annie. "Nothin' else?"

Verneice thought for a moment. "Nope, that was all she said. Why? Don't tell me you were expecting her to ask about you and the kids. Girl, she don't care nothin' about y'all. You know that."

Annie knew that.

"Well, then, what's eatin' you?" she asked.

Annie was embarrassed to admit to her neighbor that there wasn't a lot of food in the house, and there certainly wouldn't be anything to eat in a few days. She took a deep breath, let out a sigh, and told Verneice how concerned she was about feeding the kids.

Verneice knew that Annie wouldn't take money from her. She wasn't even sure if Annie knew what a dollar looked like or even how to count.

She glanced at the open window in Annie's kitchen and remembered the pecan pie that sat there yesterday.

"Say," said Verneice, "you got enough pecans to cook up two pies for me today? I'll pay you for them."

Annie smiled. "Sure, we've got a whole barrel from Mama D's property that's down by the cotton gin."

"Got any flour in the house?" Verneice asked.

"Yep, Mama D brought home two big bags right before the ice storm last winter," replied Annie.

"Sugar?"

"Yep."

"Corn syrup?"

"Yep."

"Okay," said Verneice, "we're in business. I'm having a makeup party tonight at my house and I need some dessert. Instead of baking them myself, I'll buy them from you. Then you can take the money and buy you some vittles." She reached out to shake Annie's hand.

They shook hands, but Annie wasn't reacting quite the way Verneice thought she should be after such a fine deal. "What's wrong, Annie? Why are you set to cryin', honey?"

Annie paused for a moment then answered. "Will you show me how to buy our food with that money yore givin' me?"

Verneice reached out and cupped Annie's face with her manicured hands. "Of course, sweetie. Now get in there and bake me some pies!"

They both laughed. Annie turned toward her house.

"Oh, sweetie," Verneice said. "Just one more thing. I can't quite put my finger on it, but there's something different about you."

"I don't rightly know what that could be, Mis' Verneice. "I'm just the same ol' person I've always been."

"That's it!" Verneice shrieked. "You talk different! Your English is better. You don't talk so country anymore. Why?"

Annie knew exactly what she meant. The boys had even remarked that their mama talked different. She sensed it, too, and decided to share her secret of the book with Verneice.

"Why, I've taught myself to read, Mis' Verneice. That's the only thing I can figure. But please don't tell Mama D or Daddy Jack or anybody. Please?"

"Your secret's safe with me, honey." Then they shook hands again and parted ways. As Annie approached the steps to the back porch, Dub pulled up into the gravel driveway in his truck. He hollered to Annie and she waved back, and he could see Verneice's backside walking to her house.

"Say, that Mis' Verneice ain't causin' you any trouble, is she?" he asked.

Annie shook her head. "She just ordered two pecan pies from me, Dub."

"Pies? You in the pie-making business now?"

"I am today," Annie replied. "C'mon inside and I'll get you a piece. Want some coffee, too?"

Dub followed her into the house. He saw the kids sitting in the living room watching TV and was taken off guard.

"I don't reckon I've ever seen those kids in the living room b'fore. And I sure don't recollect them ev'r watchin' no television."

"Times are a'changin'," said Annie, as she poured Dub a cup of coffee and slid a piece of pie onto a plate. "By the way, Dub, Mama D wants you to come get the hogs and take them to your place 'til they get back from Herndon."

"Guess they plan to be there awhile," answered Dub.

Annie nodded. "Yeah, Robert's bad off and they are staying at Helen's until they can bring him home. They tried to call you but you weren't home."

"Bet you like that a lot," said Dub.

Annie looked at him, not knowing exactly what he meant. Did he mean she liked that Robert was not doing well or that they weren't coming home anytime soon?

Dub cleared his throat. "I mean, I bet you like havin' this house to yourself."

"Oh, that," Annie replied. "Yes, it's been really nice."

Dub changed the subject. "Why'd Verneice ask you to bake two pies?"

"She needs a dessert for her party tonight and I need money to buy food," Annie answered. "We worked out a deal."

Dub sipped his coffee and tasted the pecan pie. "Does that mean you'll cook other things for money, too? Like maybe that great squirrel stew?"

"I don't know," replied Annie. "I guess so."

"With baking powder biscuits?"

"Yeah, I guess I could do that," she replied, smiling. "Why, Mr. Dub, you wouldn't know of anyone who'd like to buy my stew or biscuits, do you?"

"Yes, ma'am, I do," he said. "Me."

"And just what are you gonna do with all that food, being a single man and all?"

"Well," Dub replied, "I could take it to the cotton gin and feed some of the workers. After I get my share of it first, mind you. Those boys, they get mighty hungry at the gin, and they ain't ever tasted anything as good as your cookin', Annie. Why, you should see some of the pitiful vittles they bring to eat. Times are tough, Annie. I don't have to tell you that."

"Like what kind of vittles do they bring?"

"Oh, all kinds of meats that don't look fit for eatin'. They wrap them up in newspaper with some dried out old bread. Don't know where they get the newspaper, cuz they shore don't know how to read."

Annie thought Dub's gesture of bringing food to the gin was just the thing he'd do. Besides running Cook's ambulance service and carrying people to the hospital, Dub often helped out at the cotton gin. Right now the workers were getting the place ready for pickin' time, and things were pretty busy. Dub was also the guy you'd call if your car needed to be pulled out of a ditch, if you needed a ride to church or if your hogs needed tended to.

"And just when did you want this stew?" Annie asked.

"Hmmmmmm . . . let's see," Dub thought, scratching his beard. "Monday? Is that too soon? I don't want to cause you no inconvenience or anything. I'll pay you a good price."

"Pay me?" Annie asked. "Pay me? After all you've done for me, and now you're takin' the hogs? I don't think I could take money from you, Dub."

"Well then I won't be needin' any squirrel stew. I only want it if I can pay you. What goes on between me and the Bartons is between me and them. Takin' you and the boy up to Herndon, that's my job. So I see it this way, Mis' Annie, you and I are even."

He got up from the table, put his cap on and reached for the doorknob to the back porch to let himself out.

"Okay, Dub. Monday."

"Don't forget the biscuits," he replied, winking one eye.

"And don't forget to go squirrelin'. I'll need it by Sunday night."

"Deal," he said smiling. "That's when I'll come for the hogs."

"Deal."

21 / VERNEICE

Mama D ended her call in the pay phone booth and walked back to sit next to Daddy Jack in the hospital's waiting room. She plopped down next to him and hung her head low on her breasts. He could tell she wasn't happy about having to call Verneice, but those hogs were worth a lot of money.

"Waal?" he asked.

"Waal, whut?" she answered gruffly.

"Did you git Verneice?"

"Yeah, she wuz thar."

"So whut's eatin' you? Why you in sech a hissy?"

Mama D raised her head slowly, her eyes rolling to the right at Daddy Jack, her nose snorting like a bull ready for attack. She began talking in a loud whisper, grinding her teeth as she spoke.

"Whut's eatin' me? Whut's eatin' me? You got some gall astin' that. You know damned well whut's eatin' me. Why, I n'ver thought I'd have to ast that bitch for a favor."

"Okay, okay. Whut else was we suppos'd to do? It's not like we got a phone in the house or nuthin.' Can't depend on Dub for everthang. Them hogs gotta be fed."

"Oh, to hell with yer damned hogs!" she said loudly, nudging Daddy Jack in the arm with her elbow.

A woman sitting across from them in the waiting room raised her head from her book, removed her reading glasses and gave Mama D a stare that could paralyze a hound dog.

Daddy Jack caught the woman's eyes on them. "Shhhhhhhhhh," Daddy Jack said. "Jest shhhhhhhh."

Mama D didn't let up. "You shoulda heered her, that's all," she said through gritted teeth. "She wuz squawkin' like a hawk 'bout to gut a dead rabbit, goin' on an' on 'bout how she couldn't b'leeve I wuz callin' her, and wait 'til she tells her makeup girls tonight. Why, I'm jest gonna be a laughin' stock in Cook."

Daddy Jack slumped in his chair and let out a big sigh.

After Verneice hung up the phone from talking to Mama D, she couldn't stop giggling. She walked into the bathroom and unrolled the bristle curlers from her hair, tossing them one-by-one into a plastic container inside a drawer under the sink. She looked at herself in the huge wall mirror and a smug face looked back.

"Gotcha, Mama D!" she said sarcastically, waving both her hands with furled fingers that resembled guns. "It's time you got down off that high horse and acknowledged my existence."

She shook her head to fluff the curls, ran her fingers through the strands like a comb, pulled it up into a French Twist topped with curls, and sprayed it with Aqua Net. "Time to celebrate your comeuppance," she said, grabbing a tube of lipstick and smearing its ruby red color on her mouth. Puckering, she smirked, "That'll teach ya." Then she mimicked a kiss at her image and turned toward the kitchen to pour a jigger of Jack Daniels.

The hatred for each other had been smoldering for years. Verneice always suspected that it was Mama D who got the tongues wagging about her back in 1943. Even though Doc Wilks took a vow of confidentiality with his patients, word always got out somehow. Gossip hit the air like a radio broadcast, and the folks in Cook would devour it as fast as buzzards in a hog gut factory.

It wasn't something she was proud of, that's for sure, but she didn't need everyone to know about it. It all started when the Army set up a facility outside of Herndon to train B-17 bomber pilots and crewmen. More than 6,000 soldiers came to Tennessee, and Herndon's nightlife picked up significantly. Every Friday and Saturday night Verneice and her best friend,

Alice, would drive into town to Sam's Saloon and other watering holes and drink and dance with members of the U.S. military.

During the two years that the base was an active facility, Verneice was like a kid in a candy store, savoring the taste of sweet soldiers and spitting the sour ones out.

She was gone for days at a time, worrying her mother, Maydell, and causing problems for many of the married soldiers whose wives would come to visit. Doc Wilks treated her for gonorrhea, syphilis, crabs, and urinary tract infections. She was blamed for spreading the diseases to many of the men on base and was barred from several clubs in Herndon. No matter how hard her mother threatened or pleaded, Verneice didn't let up from her partying – until she got pregnant.

The man she accused of knocking her up was a naïve hick from Arkansas. He vowed to take care of her and the baby, but he wanted to send her to his parents' farm until his time was up in the Army. She refused, asking for money instead.

The thought of having an illegitimate baby under her roof was the last straw for Maydell. The revered schoolteacher, who had helped so many students with numerous learning and economic difficulties, couldn't take any more from her daughter. She packed up Verneice and drove her to the bus station to live in Kentucky with Maydell's older sister. But while they were waiting in the bus station, Verneice hunched over in pain, and blood ran down her leg. Doc Wilks couldn't save the fetus from aborting, and Maydell insisted he sterilize her daughter. A reluctant Verneice agreed.

While Verneice recuperated, Maydell discovered several envelopes from soldiers in the drawers of her daughter's dresser. Each soldier had pleaded with Verneice in his letter not to tell his wife that she was pregnant, and each had enclosed a check as hush money. This discovery put even more of a strain on the mother-daughter relationship, and Maydell confided in her childhood friend, Mama D.

Verneice, her once beautiful daughter, a delightful child and well liked by many, was now a ruthless scam artist with no morals. What had she done wrong? She was quick to blame Verneice's father, Verne Stokes, because his side of the family had the sickness – generations of alcoholism and mental illness. But she didn't like to talk ill of the dead.

"God will judge him fairly," she'd always say when people around her blamed him for Verneice's ways.

Whatever it was, Maydell wasn't having any more of it. She set down strict rules for Verneice to follow. The free ride was over, Maydell told her daughter, and insisted she find a job or leave. She worked multiple menial jobs until finding a good fit. An ad in the Herndon newspaper for saleswomen for a door-to-door cosmetics company changed her life. The minute the executives laid eyes on her they knew she was a good fit.

"Wait until the girls hear about Miss High and Mighty groveling for my help," Verneice said aloud after kicking back another shot of whiskey.

"This'll be a makeup party like no other."

22 / THE WAIT

Daddy Jack stared at the waiting room door that led to the hospital rooms, watching for Dr. Shea to emerge with news about Robert's condition. Earlier, the doctor told the Bartons to make arrangements to stay in Herndon until Robert's condition was stable. He had a massive infection and a high fever, and it would take a few days before the medicine took effect. He was no longer in a regular hospital bed, but in a special unit for people with serious illnesses, and his parents weren't allowed up there just any time they wanted to go.

Dr. Shea postponed his trip to California to treat Robert's infection. It wasn't like he cared for the man personally, but Robert was Annie's husband and he was committed to healing the sick. He disliked Robert's parents, but was concerned about Annie's kids. Being raised without a father is something he knew firsthand, and he had no idea what would happen to Annie if her husband died.

Mama D's sister opened her house in Herndon to the Bartons and told them they could stay as long as they needed. Helen's kids were grown and gone and she was a widow, so there was plenty of room and lots of clothes for Daddy Jack to wear. She didn't allow whiskey or tobacco in the house, but Daddy Jack was used to that. He was like a magician when it came to hiding bottles and smokes, and then pulling them out at just the right moment for a swig or a puff without anyone suspecting a thing.

Daddy Jack squirmed in the uncomfortable waiting room chair until he found a suitable sleeping position. Mama D finally settled down after her call to Verneice, and her mind returned to thoughts of Robert, her only child and the only person she had ever truly loved, except for his real daddy, of course.

"God," she prayed to herself, "I knowed I done a lot of cruel thangs in my life, but I already lost his daddy. You cain't take my boy, too. It jest wouldn't be right to take 'em both from me."

In her eyes, Jack was no substitute for Minner and never would be. Robert's daddy was a town favorite, a rooster of a fella, who liked to fish, hunt, work hard and make love to her every night. She and Minner had five years with each other before she got pregnant with Robert. Neither one of them could understand how that could happen because of all the times they'd had sex. Each one suspected something physical was wrong with the other one, but never said it out loud.

But at 19, Mama D delivered a healthy baby boy, 8 lbs. 8 oz., perfect head and a long body, with Minner's big feet and hands. They showed him off proudly at church every Sunday, and Mama D and her beautiful baby son were a common sight to see at Tinker's Tow where the townspeople would make over him and tell Minner what a lucky man he was.

Mama D was radiant and alive, living a fairy-tale life that all little girls in Cook dreamed about while growing up. She laughed a lot back then, told a lot of funny jokes and was prettier than Herndon's Cotton Queen.

No one called her Mama D. Minner affectionately called her "Dot," short for her birth name, Dorthea. She loved to hear him call her that. Sometimes he'd say "Dotsie" or "Dotty" and even called her "Dotsie Doodle" during their romps in bed.

"Who loves you, Dotsie Doodle?" he'd say in her face, panting and almost out of breath on top of her after a round of lovemaking. "Who's crazy mad for you, huh?" he'd say.

It didn't matter what he called her. She loved the sound of her name across his lips any way he wanted to say it.

It was Daddy Jack who gave her the nickname "Mama D." It went well with "Daddy Jack," the name she chose for Robert to call him. She was never going to let Robert forget his real daddy. No one was going to take Minner's place in Robert's life. So 'daddy' or 'pa' or 'dad' was out of the question, although he'd slip from time to time and blurt out 'Paw,' only to meet with an evil stare from his mother.

Daddy Jack wasn't real clear about a lot of Mama D's thinking, but he knew what was going on with the name thing. He also knew about the numerous pet names that Minner used to call her because he overheard them a time or two before he died.

Early in their marriage, Daddy Jack slipped and called her "Dot" while she was at the stove cooking. She flew into a rage at the sound of "Dot" coming from Jack's mouth and threw a hot pan of grease his way. The skillet landed on the floor, splashing his leg and burning his skin through his overalls. The next day he started calling her Mama D. It stuck, and there were no more slip-ups.

Now over 40, Mama D looked like an old woman far beyond her years. She knew she had a meanness that ate at her bones and caused her to age before her time and become a large fleshy, wrinkled woman. But Jack didn't seem to mind. He stuck by her no matter how bad she treated him. She often thought it was because of his debt to Minner, a debt that he rang up when the two of them were six years old and swimming in Miller's Pond – when Jack was drowning and Minner pulled him to safety.

She stared at Jack sleeping in the chair next to her in the hospital's waiting room and selfishly wished it was him in the hospital room instead of Robert. She was never attracted to Jack. *Never.* In fact, she never really liked him much even though he was Minner's best friend. She wasn't much of a wife to Jack, either, especially in the bedroom, and that was one of the reasons she brought Annie into the family.

Annie's daddy, Ernest, was a low-life drunk who owed people money all over town, including Mama D and Daddy Jack. He beat Annie's mother on a regular basis until she died in childbirth with their ninth child. Right before she died, Mama D caught Ernest cashing in three bags of pecans he had picked from her land. It was not the first time he had stolen from her property, and she threatened to call the law. He said he'd do anything to keep from going to jail. Mama D wanted Annie. He said, "Okay."

Her little scheme worked well for a while. Daddy Jack found great pleasure in Robert's new bride. Sneaking around behind Robert's and Mama D's backs to get at Annie aroused him even more. He left Mama D alone and she was a lot happier. But Annie was getting pregnant every year and it was causing a financial hardship on all of them. So Mama D ordered him to stop fooling with her.

And now, with Robert's illness, there was another big problem.

Twenty years ago when Mama D had to sell Tinker's Tow & Garage to pay Minner's debt, Minner's Uncle James paid cash for it up front. The garage continued to do well after Minner's death, but over the past few years, James hadn't been able to run the gas station and store because of his arthritis. It was run down and no one wanted to buy it in such poor condition. Then last month, unexpectedly, James died at 83, leaving the gas station and garage to Robert and Annie in his will.

If Robert dies, God forbid, that damn girl will git everthang, Mama D thought. *We gotta sell it fast.*

She looked around and saw that there was no one else in the waiting room. The old biddy who had given her the evil eye had gone home, and there weren't any nurses behind the window, either, at least that she could see. She nudged Daddy Jack from his sleep.

"C'mon, Jack, let's go. It's midnight and thar ain't nothin' we cain do here for now."

She actually just wanted to get away from all the quiet time in the waiting room that allowed her thoughts to wander to happier times with Minner. It never really did any good to think about him because it just made her hate her life now even more. Robert's illness complicated her head, too, and she was thinking too much about losing him and how she would have nothing to live for if he died.

Daddy Jack slowly rose from the chair and stretched. They both started to walk toward the exit for their short drive to Helen's when Dr. Shea entered the waiting room.

"There's no change, Mr. and Mrs. Barton. I'm very sorry," he said from across the room. "I'm leaving now myself. I guess I'll see you tomorrow?"

They shrugged their shoulders and kept on walking.

23 / THE GROCERY STORE

The pies were a big hit at Verneice's makeup party and Annie received three more orders. Verneice gave her 50 cents per pie and told Annie she'd walk up to the store with her to help buy groceries.

The store wasn't anything like Annie imagined. The hardwood floors were old and sprinkled with sawdust. Several loud fans were blowing the warm air around that smelled like a mixture of apples, tobacco, and mold.

The wooden shelves were warped and half-filled with canned and bottled goods, boxed items, work tools, overalls and shirts, material for making clothes, thread, and lots of different sizes of nails.

Baskets of various fruits and vegetables lined a long table in front of the window. Flies were everywhere, but more so on the huge barrel of apples.

In a refrigerator case with glass doors, Annie could see cartons of milk, Rag Bologna, cheese, eggs and bottled chocolate drinks. She watched a young man enter the store, walk over to a huge, red tin box and lift up its heavy lid. Curious, she walked closer to see what was inside. She saw the caps on rows and rows of cold bottled drinks, and the sweaty man maneuvered the one he wanted through a channel to the end of a row, clanging other bottles on its way. When it got to the end, he pulled the neck of the bottle straight up and out of the box. Then he inserted the top of the bottle into a small hole on the side of the box and flipped off its cap. The bottle's contents fizzed and dripped down its side, and the man drew it up to his mouth and gulped down the liquid without stopping to take a breath.

"My stars, he sure is thirsty!" remarked Annie to the boys.

Then the man went through the process again for another one, and left with it unopened.

In a corner at the back of the store, a large man stood in a tiny room putting envelopes in slots on the wall. Annie could see him through a window-like opening that was covered with black bars. She wondered if that was the mailroom she'd heard about, and was puzzled by the iron bars. She walked down the store's aisles with Becky in her arms and both boys clasping her sundress. Verneice led the way.

"One year around Easter time this whole store chirped like a hatchery," Verneice said excitedly. "Folks ordered these little chicks from a catalog and they all came in at once. Some of 'em got loose and people were scramblin' all over the store to get 'em back in their boxes. It was a sight to see, all right."

Annie smiled at the thought of little chicks running around on the dusty hardwood floors and tiny feathers flying everywhere.

"Now, see these numbers?" Verneice asked, pointing to a price sticker. "That's how much you pay for it. If it says forty-nine, that means forty-nine cents, almost half of your dollar bill."

Annie nodded. She knew numbers, maybe not as good as Verneice who had schooling, but she knew a little. The book taught her how to add, subtract and divide. The fractions part was a little hard to understand at first, but the book showed her samples of pies that were divided into all kinds of pieces, and she got a better feel for those kinds of numbers because of the pictures.

Annie saw things on the store's shelves that she never knew existed. "What's this?" she asked Verneice.

"Sanitary napkins," replied Verneice, trying to smother a chuckle of embarrassment.

"For the kitchen?" Annie asked.

"Oh, lordy, no," Verneice giggled out loud, looking around the store to see if anyone was within earshot. All eyes were on them, staring at Annie and the kids like they were creatures from another planet. But no one was near enough to hear their conversation.

"Annie," Verneice whispered, "when you bleed every month, what do you use to keep the blood from getting on your clothes?"

Annie's face turned red. She put her head down and whispered back. "I use these old rags Mama D gave me."

Dumbfounded, Verneice asked, "Do you throw them out every time?"

"Oh, no!" said Annie. "I wash them."

Verneice cocked her head and stared at Annie with a curious look. "And just how do these rags stay between your legs?"

"I pin them to my drawers," said Annie.

"Well, I'll be!" exclaimed Verneice. "How uncomfortable! Here, let me buy you some of these. On me. They take the place of rags and then you just throw them out."

Annie's face lit up with a big smile. "I just throw them out?"

"Yep. And you don't even use pins. You use this belt with two clips. I'll show you later, okay, hon?"

"Okay!" said Annie.

Verneice scooped up two boxes of sanitary napkins and put them on the store's counter. The men sitting on the front porch peered through the opened door and windows at the two women. A warm breeze flowed in from outside, along with the men's tobacco scent.

"Say, now, Mis' Verneice, who's that gal you done brought with you today?" asked the store's owner, Clyde Tubbs.

"Why, Mr. Tubbs, this here is Annie Barton," replied Verneice, in a sweet, flirty tone. "Annie, this here is Mr. Clyde Tubbs, the owner of the store and Cook's postmaster."

"Hello," answered Annie, recognizing the man that she had just seen minutes earlier through the iron window at the back of the store. Her boys peeked from behind her skirt to take a look at the man.

"Hello," said Clyde. "Who you got behind ya?"

"Oh, those are my boys, Dwayne and Will. They are kinda shy. This here is Becky."

Becky let out a squeal and a big smile when she spied the jar of cookies on the counter. Her arm stretched out and her little fingers opened and closed, motioning Annie to give her one.

Clyde picked three from the jar. "Is this what you want, little one?" he said holding up one of the cookies.

Becky jumped up and down on Annie's hip and her arm stretched as far as she could extend it.

"And what about your brothers? Think they might want one, too?" Clyde asked Becky.

Dwayne and Will came out from behind Annie's skirt and nodded.

"Well, here you go then," said Clyde, handing each one a cookie.

"Thank you, sir," said Annie. "That is so nice of you to share your food with my children."

Clyde smiled at her. "And what can I get for you today, young lady?"

"I have money to pay for my things," replied Annie. "I have a dollar and I need milk, cereal and canned soup."

"We've got all that," said Clyde. "Say, are you the one who makes the delicious pecan pies?"

Annie looked surprised and glanced over at Verneice.

"My wife was at Verneice's last night and she said she ordered a pie from Verneice's neighbor. Said it was the best pecan pie she'd ever eaten. You that neighbor?"

Annie bobbed her head.

"Well, listen. How 'bout you cook up some real small pecan pies, like maybe in a muffin pan. Yeah, like that size. Then wrap them up in wax paper and I'll sell them for a nickel. I'll give you three cents for each one and I'll make two. How's that sound? You interested?"

Annie thought a minute. That was a lot of work, she thought, and a lot of money to spend making them. Using an example she remembered from the book, she calculated in her head how much it would cost to buy all the ingredients, then divvy it up into small portions. Right now, she got fifty cents for a whole pie, but if she cut that pie in half, then cut those halves in half, and each of those parts in half, she'd have eight portions. Each portion would be enough to fill a muffin slot. So eight muffins times three cents would mean just 24 cents a pie. No, she'd have to have more.

"Sell them for 10 cents a muffin pie and give me seven cents," she said. "You get three."

"You got a deal, Mrs. Barton," said Clyde, reaching across the counter to shake her hand.

"And throw in the waxed paper, too, okay?" she pleaded. "I don't have enough money for that right now."

"I'll throw that in for free," said Clyde. "Every new customer gets a free item around here." He winked at Verneice and placed the paper in a bag, then went around the store to gather up her groceries.

"That'll be one dollar even," Clyde said after he rang up her order.

Annie gave him the money. "When did you want those muffin pies?" she asked.

"When can you get them to me?"

"I'll bake them today, along with the pies that your wife and two other ladies ordered. I'll bring them to you tomorrow," Annie replied.

"That sounds good," said Clyde.

"And you will pay me tomorrow, too?" Annie asked boldly.

"Yep. Payment on demand," he said.

"Good," Annie said. "There's some other things around here I need."

Annie was giddy during the walk home and Verneice was the quiet one for a change. She rambled on and on about what all she was going to do, how she was going to do it, and then asked, "What if the smaller pies don't sell?"

"Don't worry about that, honey. They'll sell. You know, you really surprised me back there! I had no idea you had such a head for business. Must be all that readin' you're doin'."

"Must be," said Annie.

As soon as they put the groceries up and had lunch, she and the boys shelled pecans until their fingers hurt. When the children were down for their afternoon nap, Annie made the whole pies, and then the smaller ones in an old muffin tin she found at the back of one of the kitchen cupboards. Dub came by unexpectedly and brought a skinned squirrel.

"You're not supposed to come until tomorrow!" she scolded. "I'm right in the middle of cooking pies!"

"I know, I know," said Dub, apologetically. "Clyde told me about your pies. You don't have to cook the stew tonight. The meat will keep in the refrigerator until tomorrow."

Since Dub was there she decided to put him to work and sent him to the garden to pull up onions and carrots. The potatoes weren't ready, but she had a few store-bought ones on the back porch.

Dub washed the vegetables and cut up the squirrel. Then he wrapped the meat in the wax paper and placed it in the refrigerator.

"Thanks, Dub," Annie said. "It's nice to have help."

Dub paused and chose his words carefully. "I'd do anything for you, Annie," he said.

"*Anything.*"

24 / THE DEED

The next week was the busiest of Annie's entire life. Her large pecan pies and small muffin pies were selling like hotcakes at Clyde's store. He couldn't keep them in stock and had to start a waiting list of names. In just five days, Annie made nine dollars.

The men at the cotton gin lapped up the squirrel stew and wanted more. Dub gave her two dollars for the pot and her baking powder biscuits, and placed another order, this time for fried chicken. He said he'd bring the chicken by and clean it up just like he did the squirrel.

Annie's children acted like angels while she baked. It rained off and on all week and they were inside the house most of the time, but the television provided lots of entertainment. Dwayne and Will cracked pecans for her, and Annie pushed Becky's crib up to the door of the kitchen so the baby could watch all the activity. Only once during the week did the four of them make it out to the creek to read the book, but that was all right. Annie was learning a lot about the world from the TV's ten o'clock news.

Dub brought word about Robert's condition every time he drove his ambulance to Herndon, which was about twice a week. Robert was still in a coma, and Mama D and Daddy Jack were half out of their minds with worry, and half out of their minds with having to put up with each other. One afternoon when Dub was driving away from the hospital with a patient, Mama D flagged him down. He rolled down the window, wondering what favor she wanted him to do for her this time.

"Say, now, Dub, you think you might want to buy Tinker's Tow?" she asked. "It's for sale, ya know."

"Oh, yeah?" Dub replied. "Who says?"

"Me, that's who, you ol' fart. James done give it back in his will."

"Well, I'll be. How much you want?"

"Waal," Mama D thought for a second, "I don't rightly know. But yer interested, ain't ya?"

"Could be."

"Only one thang keepin' it from bein' yern," Mama D whispered. She leaned down into the driver's side window and rested her arm on the door. "Robert, he ain't waked up yet, so he cain't sign yet, but Annie, her name's on the paper, too. Git her to sign the damn thang over to Robert and I'll cut ya a good deal. The lawyer done wrote up a special letter for that to hap'n. She jest needs to sign it."

Dub always knew Mama D was a conniving woman, but he had never witnessed it firsthand. He'd heard about her shenanigans from others she had duped over the years. Asking him to do something against the law that involved Annie was NOT going to happen. He had no intention of getting Annie to sign away something that was legally hers, but he agreed in order to get his hands on the document.

"Okay," Dub said. "I'll see what I can do."

Mama D raced back into the waiting room and came back with a stuffed envelope. Dub took it and shoved it in the ambulance's glove box.

"Gotta do it quick," Mama D said. "Time's ah runnin' out. I got other offers."

"Gotcha," said Dub, steering the ambulance away from the hospital and toward the direction of Cook.

"That ol' biddy," Dub said to himself. "I can't wait to see the look on Annie's face when I show her this."

The trip back from Herndon took forever for Dub, probably because he was anxious to get to Annie's. He had to deliver his passenger first, then clean up the ambulance, get his truck, and stop at his house before going to her house. He arrived at Annie's just as she was taking some pies out of the oven.

"Don't tell me you've brought that chicken over already!" Annie said when she saw Dub on the other side of the screen door. "I don't need it for two more days."

"Naw, Annie, I know that," he said, blushing. He always got that way around her, like a high school kid weak in the knees at the sight of a pretty girl. "I need to talk to you for a minute, if I can. And I got this heer critter for you to cook instead of the chicken – but not today, so don't get upset."

Dub took three packages of cleaned and wrapped squirrel out of a paper bag for her to see.

"That's just *one* squirrel?" she asked, looking at the large quantity of wrapped meat.

"Yeah," Dub replied. "He was a big'un, 'bout as big as a 'possum, he was."

"Okay, bring it on in and put it in the refrigerator. Want some coffee?"

"Naw."

"Okay, then. What do you want to talk about?"

Dub sat with his hands together on the table and fiddled with a toothpick he'd taken from his mouth. "Well, I don't know how to tell you this, Annie, but you own some property in this town and Mama D wants to sell it behind yer back."

Annie pushed back the chair, got up and started walking around the kitchen. She put her hands to her head and rubbed both temples. She looked at Dub. "I own *property*?"

"Yup. Tinker's Tow."

"But that's Robert's uncle's place!"

"Not anymore!" Dub said. "The old man died and left it to you and Robert. But Robert's in a coma. He's dead to the world. Cain't do a thing, not even pee on his own. I figure Mama D's goin' to sign his name on the deed and she wants me to git you to sign a paper that says you don't want the property."

"What?" Annie asked.

"Yeah, and she wants *me* to buy it," Dub answered.

Annie walked back to the table and slumped in the chair. "Tell me the truth, Dub. What did you say? Did you say you'd get me to sign it?" Her eyes welled with tears.

Dub reached over and took her hand from her lap. "I did, Annie, but only because I wanted her to give me the deed so we could look it over. I'd never do anythang behind your back."

Annie sat upright in the chair. She believed him. Her gut told her he was telling the truth. Not many people passed her gut test.

"Okay, let's look at the paper," she said excitedly.

Dub went to his truck and got the envelope out of the glove box. He brought it inside and they opened it together. Along with the deed to Tinker's Tow & Garage was a copy of James' will stating that in the event of his death, Robert and Annie Barton would take over ownership of the gas station and attached mart known as the Tinker's Tow & Garage, previously owned by Robert's father, Minner Brown. Another paper was typed up for Annie's signature, which would relinquish her rights to the property if she signed it.

They looked at each other and laughed like two little kids who'd just found a sack of money. They stopped suddenly when they heard Verneice screaming and banging on the screen door.

"Annie! Annie! Open up the door!" she yelled.

Annie hurried to the door and unlocked the screen. "What? What's wrong?"

Verneice, out of breath and her face flushed and sweaty, could hardly get the words out.

"It's Robert," she said. "Mama D just called and said he's dead." Then she broke down and sobbed.

Verneice's tears surprised Annie. She wondered why her neighbor was showing so much emotion over her husband.

"Do you want to come in, Verneice? Have a cup of coffee?" Annie asked.

"No, I need to get home and take a pill and lay down."

Annie watched Verneice walk away with her head down and shoulders slumped, fighting to stay upright on her wobbly feet.

Puzzled, Annie turned around and walked back into the kitchen.

25 / THE LIGHTER

Daddy Jack could hardly see the road through his wet eyes as he guided the truck back to Cook with trembling hands. A fatigued Mama D sat next to him with her head on his right shoulder and her eyes closed, but dry.

When Dr. Shea came out to the waiting room to tell them that Robert had died, Mama D grabbed her heart and fell back in the chair. She looked at Daddy Jack like she had seen a ghost, her mouth open and her eyes as huge as silver dollars. But she didn't cry. She didn't holler or cuss or throw a tantrum. She just stared with blank eyes. Dr. Shea told Daddy Jack that she could be in shock and to take her home and put her to bed.

"We'll take care of everything on this end," said Dr. Shea. "We just need to know what funeral home to call."

Mama D's heart raced when she heard Dr. Shea say *funeral*, and she sighed and moaned. They hadn't thought about burying Robert, only about bringing him home alive and well. Daddy Jack only knew one funeral home — the one that took care of Minner.

"Baker and Sons over on Willett Street," he told Dr. Shea.

The doctor nodded. "I am so sorry for your loss, sir."

"Thank you, doctor." They shook hands and the Bartons left the hospital for home, not even stopping at Helen's to grab their belongings. They just wanted to go home.

Annie knew they'd be coming soon and she didn't know what to expect. Would Mama D throw a hissy and toss her and the kids out? Or would she allow them to at least stay until the funeral was over? She thought about several ways the situation could go and decided to prepare for the worst.

Shortly after the hysterical Verneice had banged on Annie's back door and screamed that Robert had died, Dub hightailed it to Herndon. Annie already had a feeling that this day was coming, and she had a plan. *If they come home and kick me and the kids out, they won't give me time to get all my things together.*

She called the boys into the living room. With Becky sitting in her lap, Will and Dwayne took a seat on the couch on each side of her. They knew something was wrong by the look on her face and the tone of her voice, and they were quiet and attentive.

"Boys," she began softly, "you know your daddy was real sick with that bad sore. Well, it got really bad and his body couldn't fight the poison off, so God took your daddy to live in Heaven forever. He won't be coming home here no more, and I don't really know if Mama D and Daddy Jack will let us live in this house no more without him."

Dwayne ran his fingers up and down Annie's arm to console her. Will sucked his thumb and beat his feet against the couch. Becky squirmed in Annie's lap and pulled at her right breast, summoning her supper. Annie lifted up her top and she started sucking.

"Anyway, boys, we don't have much time. If Mama D and Daddy Jack want us out, then we gotta go. But I want us to take all we can."

She told the boys to go to their room, get their pillowcases off their bed and stuff them with all their clothes. She said she would do the same, and crammed everything of hers and all of Becky's things, too, into a pillowcase.

They worked fast, opening drawers and shoveling out clothes into the cases, trying to leave enough fabric at the end to tie a knot. Annie went to the pantry and took cans of food that she had bought with her own money and a box of crackers. She put those in a grocery sack that Clyde had given her. They left Becky in the crib for just a few minutes while they walked their bundles out to the barn. She was halfway there when she remembered the deed.

"Dang! I forgot somethin', boys. Just stay right here and I'll be back lickety-split."

She ran up the back porch's steps, threw open the door and lunged toward the kitchen table to grab the envelope that was sitting in the center. Then off she ran to catch up with the boys.

The barn was up off the ground on concrete blocks about two feet high in case Pig Dog Creek overflowed and flooded their land. Annie chose a spot under the back right corner to deposit their belongings, but she didn't want to lay the pillowcases right on top of the moist dirt. She looked around to see if there was anything she could put down first, and saw a large cardboard box that Robert had used to carry beans from one of the fields. She flattened the box and put the clothes on top of it.

With the clothes secure, they ran back to the house and gathered up the small pecan pies to take next door. They rang Verneice's doorbell, but she didn't answer right away. They were just about to leave when they heard her unlatch the chain inside and turn the knob. The door opened slowly and she stuck her tousled head forward.

"Oh . . . hello. What's goin' on?" she said groggily, like she had just awakened from a deep sleep. Her breath hinted of whiskey. Her lips stuck together slightly.

"I'm sorry to bother you, Verneice, but I need you to take these pies to Clyde for me, if you would," Annie said. "Mama D and Daddy Jack are coming home right quick and I don't want them to know that I've been bakin' for the store. Can you do that for me?"

Verneice shook her head like she was trying to wake up and understand the question. She banged the right palm of her hand against the right temple of her head as if to get rid of the ringing inside her skull.

"Oh . . . sure, hon. Bring 'em on in."

Verneice opened the door wider for them to enter and a blast of cold air hit the boys and Annie by surprise. The three of them huddled together and walked slowly inside the air-conditioned house, following her to the kitchen and admiring the shiny paneling, painted pictures and pretty knickknacks along the way.

"Just set them down here," she said, making room on her turquoise countertop. "I'll take 'em up to the store for ya. I gotta go up there anyhow to get something . . . oh, yeah, milk. Mama needs milk."

It was the first time that Verneice had mentioned her mother in a conversation. Annie often wondered about Maydell and her health. If she wasn't right in the head anymore, like she had overheard Mama D say one day to Robert, where did Verneice put her mother when the women came over to her makeup parties?

"Is your mother home?" asked Annie politely.

Verneice closed her eyes and leaned against the sink to catch her balance. "What?" she asked.

"Your mother, Verneice. Is she home?" Annie asked again.

Verneice grabbed the back of her neck with her right hand and rubbed it. "Lord, I can't even think straight 'cuz of that pill I took. Wha'd you say, hon?"

"Oh, nothing," said Annie. She arranged the pies nicely on the counter and made sure the wax paper was secure around them so they wouldn't dry out. The kitchen was beautiful and sparkly clean, with turquoise counters and white cabinets accented with black handles. There wasn't a stove, but instead there were four coiled burners on the top of one of the counters, and a turquoise oven was set in a white-bricked wall.

The floor was covered with squares of vinyl that were wheat-colored and surrounded by white strips. A huge, iron wall hanging painted turquoise held hanging pots and pans, its coil shapes matching the black accents on the cabinets.

Annie had never seen a kitchen like that before, but there was one area that looked really familiar – the kitchen table. It was decorated with plates and napkins similar to the table she had seen in her book, and she smiled when she spotted the cute little tomato-shaped salt and pepper shaker set. But in-between the shakers and just barely out of sight was an object that she hadn't seen in a very long time. When she took a step toward the table to see it better without arousing any suspicion from Verneice, she recognized it as Robert's lighter.

It had belonged to his father, and Mama D gave it to Robert on his 16th birthday. Minner had found it wedged in the front seat of his new Hudson the day after he purchased the car in Memphis, the same car that he was driving when he was decapitated. It was a silver-colored Zippo with a Greyhound Lines insignia on top, one of the first Zippo lighters decorated with a company's insignia.

Annie's thoughts went crazy for a minute as she tried to understand how Robert's lighter had found its way into Verneice's house.

Did Verneice take it from the Bartons' house? No, she couldn't have because she's never been inside. Did Robert give it to her? No! Why would he give such a precious item to her? He loved that lighter! Or maybe Robert left it here?

Then it hit her.

Robert and Verneice were seeing each other! No wonder she was so upset over his death! No wonder she took the pill and can't think clearly. Good God! Verneice and Robert? Mrs. Clean and Mr. Dirty? How could that be? But Mama D must've known and that's why she hates her so and calls her a whore all the time!

Dwayne pulled at Annie's shirt. "Let's go, Mama."

"Uhhhh . . . Verneice, we've got to go now. C'mon boys."

Verneice stumbled toward the door and opened it. "Thank you," Annie said, guiding her boys out the door and onto the porch.

"My pleasure," she slurred, and slammed the door.

26 / THE KEY

The Bartons' truck pulled up alongside the house just minutes after Annie and the boys returned from the creek where they had removed the book from the log and placed it under the barn with the rest of their belongings. Annie was taking no chances with anyone – not with Verneice who knew about her ability to read, and certainly not with Mama D, who could erupt violently and banish her from the house. She was prepared for them both.

Annie reached into the refrigerator and grabbed the wrapped squirrel that Dub had left for her to cook for him. She dipped it in a shallow bowl of milk and then dredged it in flour, trying to act as if everything was normal. The clock's hands were way past eating time and she knew the Bartons would be hungry.

She no sooner sent the boys to her bedroom to watch Becky when she heard the squeak of the screen door and Mama D's and Daddy Jack's footsteps on the back porch. They opened the door to the kitchen and Annie braced herself against the stove, her heart pounding loudly, her head a little dizzy from fear.

She smelled their body odors as they entered the kitchen, a smell that she had tried to rid the house of while they were gone. Over the years their smells seeped into the walls of the old house, and soap and water wasn't strong enough to kill it. She turned from the stove to fight off harsh words or a hand that might be flying toward her, but they somberly walked past her toward their bedroom without a single word. Daddy Jack helped Mama D get into bed, then he joined Annie in the kitchen.

He pulled a chair out from the table and sat down, taking a pack of Lucky Strikes from his pocket and lighting one. Annie smelled the smoke and walked over to the kitchen cabinet to get him an ashtray. When she placed it in front of him on the table, he grabbed her arm.

"I don't know whut's gonna hap'n now, girl," he said. "Mama D ain't spoke a word since she wuz told 'bout Robert. Don't know whut it means. Don't know whut it means for you and yer young-uns neither."

Annie pulled her arm away and went over to the stove to turn the meat frying in the lard. She was afraid to say anything.

"That boy wuz like my own blood," he said softly. "It's like my own son is dead. His daddy wuz like my blood, too. You knowed he saved my life, didn't ya?"

"Yeah," Annie said in a quiet voice. She felt nothing for Daddy Jack, not even in his time of sorrow. He still was a ruthless bastard, son or no son.

"I knowed we ain't been too kind to ya, Annie, but it ain't been a good time for none of us. Not in years. I don't know how long Mama D will want ya, girl. I reckon we oughtta think 'bout whar you and the young-uns could go, jest in case . . ."

A loud knock on the front door cut Daddy Jack off in mid-sentence. He left the kitchen to answer it.

"Howdy, Larry," Daddy Jack said when he saw Sheriff Haynes standing there. "C'mon in."

Sheriff Haynes took off his cowboy hat and walked in. "How's Dorthea, Jack? She doin' all right?"

Daddy Jack glanced over to the closed bedroom door where Mama D was resting on the other side. "Naw, Larry, she ain't worth shit. She ain't said a word since Robert died. The doctor said somethang 'bout be'n in shock, whutever the hell that is."

Sheriff Haynes put his hand on Jack's shoulder. "If you need anything, Jack, just give me a holler, okay?"

"Okay."

"I gotta go now and meet up with the police in Herndon. They heard about Robert's death and the charges against Andy and Billy could be more serious now."

Daddy Jack's eyes squinted with confusion. "Why?" he asked.

"Well, Robert's death was caused by those boys. If they hadn't tarred and feathered Calvin, Robert wouldn't have gone to Miller's Pond and wrassled with that nasty boar. The new charges could be as serious as murder."

Daddy Jack ran his yellowed, nicotine-stained fingers through his greasy head and stumbled slightly. Sheriff Haynes caught him and steadied his body.

"Murder?" he gulped.

"Yeah. Not first-degree murder because they didn't kill him with their own hands, but it shore could be involuntary manslaughter. But I don't know if I'd let Dorthea know that straight away. You let me know how she's comin' along, ya hear?"

"Shore, Larry," Daddy Jack replied.

"I'll check back with you t'mara, Jack," the sheriff said, walking down the front porch's steps toward his police car.

Daddy Jack closed the door and went back to his seat at the kitchen table. "Guess you heered ever word of that, huh?" he asked Annie.

"Yeah," she answered softly. "Here, get you some food inside ya."

She gave Daddy Jack a plate of fried squirrel and potatoes. "You want some iced tea?"

"Yeah," he replied. "Whar are those young-uns? They awful quiet."

"Oh, they 'round," she said, hesitating to correct her speech in front of him. Her insides had settled down some, but her hands were still shaky.

"This shore is good," he said after about two bites of squirrel. "Whar'd this critter come from?"

"Oh, Dub brought it," she said.

"That Dub's a good man."

"Yeah, I know . . . and speaking of Dub, why I think that's him coming right now."

Annie could see Dub's ball cap rising from the steps of the back porch. He opened the screen, then made eye contact with Annie through the window of the back door. She motioned for him to come in.

"Hey, y'all," Dub said. "Am I interruptin' supper?"

"Naw," said Daddy Jack. "I'm the only one eatin.' Sit down and have ya a plate. I heered you caught this critter and brung 'em over."

Dub gave Annie a blank stare, and then realized she had fried up the squirrel he had left in the refrigerator. She turned her back to dish him up a plate from the stove.

"Yep, caught this ol' guy while squirrelin' on that land near the gin. Big ol' thang, ain't he?"

"Yep," Daddy Jack said, barely audible through a mouthful of taters.

Dub was trying to figure out Daddy Jack's mood. He nervously rambled on a minute or two bragging about how good this squirrel season had been. Daddy Jack, somber throughout the conversation, offered little in return, and Dub knew then that it was probably a safe time to talk about the arrangements he had made for Robert.

"I took care of thangs at the funeral home, Jack," he said. "Robert's service will be Monday at ten o'clock at the Baptist Church here in Cook. I can call your kinfolks for you and let them know. Clyde will spread the word, too."

Daddy Jack nodded and continued eating, only slower now.

Dub gobbled up the fried squirrel and potatoes, watching Annie's every move as he ate. He was anxious to ask her how she was doing and if she was afraid that the Bartons were going to send her away. Finally, Jack pushed his plate away, got up from the table and went into the living room. Annie put his plate in the sink and went to get her hungry boys and baby.

She brought the children out to the table and set a dinner plate in front of each of the boys. Becky was clinging to her tightly while Annie dished up their food. Then, as best she could with a heavy baby in one arm, she tore the squirrel meat away from the bones with her fingers for the boys to eat and then spread it out on their plates with the potatoes.

Dub leaned back on his chair's hind legs so he could peer into the living room. Daddy Jack was lying on the couch. He felt it was safe to talk now, but not too loudly.

"Annie, did you get the will and the deed?"

Annie nodded.

"Good girl. Is the envelope in a safe place?"

Again, Annie nodded.

"Okay, I'm gonna say this real fast, okay? Now listen up, all of y'all." He huddled over the table to talk. The boys' ears perked up.

"If for some reason y'all have to leave this house, go to the gas station. It's yours fair and square, Annie, and no one can take it from you. Do you hear?"

"Yeah, I hear," whispered Annie.

"Okay. I need you to signal to me that y'all are there somehow. Let me think a sec . . . find some kind of light and put it in the winder. Yeah, I bet ol' James had some kind of kerosene lamp or somethang inside that place. Hell, the electricity might be on for all I know. But you gotta get me word."

"Whut station, Mama?" Dwayne asked.

Annie leaned over closer to his and Will's ears and whispered loudly. "Your granddaddy owned a gas station before he died and it belongs to us now," she said. "It's just up the road. We can walk to it. Don't be afraid, okay?"

The boys perked up at the thought of living in a gas station and they made funny eyes at each other and giggled in-between bites of their food.

Dub looked at his watch. "I gotta go, Annie." His eyes met hers from across the table and he smiled. "It'll be okay. You okay?"

"Yeah. But how are we gonna get inside that place?"

"Oh! I almost forgot!" Dub said. He dug into his jeans' pocket, pulled out a key and held it up for them to see. "I found this in my glove box. It must have fallen out of the envelope. It's the key to the front door of Tinker's. I've already tried it and it works, but dammed if I didn't try the light switch to see if the electricity was on. I was in such a hurry and I didn't want anyone to see me in there."

Annie took the key from his hand and slipped it into her shoe.

"See ya, boys," Dub said, rising from the table and putting on his ball cap.

"Bye," said Will.

"See ya," said Dwayne.

Annie walked out after him, standing in the half-opened screen door with Becky on her hip. Dub stopped in the yard and turned around to see what she wanted.

"Dub, how do I get to the gas station?"

Dub put his hands on his hips and looked up at her with a big smile. "Geez, Annie, I didn't think about that! You ain't never been there a'fore, have ya?"

She was smiling, too. She didn't know why it was so funny, but it was somehow.

Dub looked around the yard. "Okay," he said, pointing to the creek. "See over yonder where Pig Dog bends to the east thatta-way?"

Annie nodded.

"Okay . . . jest follow the bank thattaway until you can see the road where the church is. That's the main road out of town. You'll know it cuz it's tarred. Walk down from the creek's bank toward the road. Go past the church and Tinker's is just a little ways down on the right."

Annie understood everything he said. "Only one thing, Dub," she said. "Does it say 'Tinkers' on the outside of the place?"

"Yeah, but the sign has fallen down. Look for the gas pump outside."

Annie knew what that was. She had seen a gas station in the book. She even knew how to spell it, but Dub didn't know that.

"Okay. Thanks, Dub." Then, after a little hesitation, she said softly, "I don't know what I'd do without you."

Her words sent goose bumps up and down his arms. He felt heat under his skin rising up his throat and covering his face. He was afraid that she could see this excitement, so he just smiled, turned abruptly, and walked to his truck. Annie watched him drive away before going back inside.

The boys were staring at her like zombies when she came through the door. "Can you believe it, boys?" she said excitedly. "We've got us a place to go and we got us a nice man to help."

They began laughing softly, nervously at first, but it felt so good after such a fitful day that it burst into a hearty release of emotion. Annie stopped suddenly when she smelled foul odor.

"Whut in the hell is so goddamn funny?" yelled Mama D, in the doorway, now fully awake and back to her old self. "Why are y'all so goddamn happy?"

Annie froze in her seat. The boys stiffened, too. Will wet his pants and the pee dripped onto the floor.

"Y'all don't even act like Robert's dead! Y'all aren't even a little bit sad a'tall!" she screamed.

Her tone got louder and louder, just as Annie suspected it would when she came to her senses. It was as if reality had finally set in for Mama D and all her pent-up anger was being released.

"WHUT KIND OF PEOPLE ARE YOU? HEATHENS, THAT'S WHUT CHA'AR. OUT!" she screamed, pointing to the back door. "GIT THE HELL OUTTA MY HOUSE AND DO IT NOW!"

Annie quickly pulled the kids away from the table and fled the kitchen through the back door. They ran to the back of the barn, pulled out their stuffed pillowcases and fled across the open field to Pig Dog Creek where she had spent many mornings bathing and reading with the kids. She knew there was probably a shortcut, but she wasn't going to take any chances of getting lost.

They followed the trees lining the creek's bank that led to the tarred road, lugging their pillowcases filled with clothes. Annie carried Becky, the book and her bundle of clothes. The boys dragged their pillowcases behind them, every now and then getting them snarled in the heavy brush. Will was barefoot, but the recent rain had created a cushion of mud for him to slosh through.

Becky put her head on Annie's shoulder and her arms around her neck and hung on. Dwayne took up the rear and kept looking back over his shoulder to make sure they weren't being followed.

They didn't have any trouble finding the tarred road or the church or Tinker's. When they reached the station, with its single gas pump and weathered sign, Annie put the key in the lock on its front door and opened it. The sun was almost down, and there was little light for them to see inside the dusty building. But Annie's eyes fixed on an old kerosene lamp on a table in the corner, just like Dub said there would be. Lying next to it was a box of matches.

She lit the lamp and placed it in the windowsill. Dub's truck pulled up outside ten minutes later.

27 / THE RAIN

A cold raindrop dripped from a tiny leak in the ceiling and landed on the bridge of Annie's nose, awakening her from a deep sleep. She shot up into a sitting position and looked around the room. It was daylight, but she had no idea what time it was. The gloomy clouds and clapping thunder made it feel more like late afternoon, but she knew it couldn't be.

The children were sleeping beside her in the bed. Dub had brought blankets with him the night before and spread them on the double bed in the bedroom behind the station.

The kerosene lamp she had placed in the front window to signal Dub put out a nice glow, and Annie and Dub had carried it throughout the building shortly after he had arrived to get a quick look at the station's condition and all that it had to offer its new tenants.

Minner's Uncle James had updated the property as soon as he bought it from Mama D. He feared the arthritis that was beginning to cripple his hands would eventually cause him to lose his house and farm land, so he sold them for a fair price and purchased the station. He remodeled the place so he could live on it. He had it all figured out. If business was slow, he'd still have a roof over his head and money in the bank from the sale of his house and land.

Dub told Annie that James lived and worked at the station for as long as he was physically able. When he couldn't feed himself anymore, he called his sister in Memphis to come get him. She drove up and James was waiting for her with his suitcase packed beside him. They locked the station's front door, got into the car, and drove off.

"No one's been back since. That's been pert near three years ago," Dub said.

After all that time, Annie knew that the place needed a good cleaning. She didn't require more light to see that. But there was something about the station that made her feel good, a warm and cozy aura that set well in her bones. She couldn't wait to see it in the daylight, with the sun coming through the windows and shining on every wall.

Large paned windows enclosed the front lobby of the gas station where an old cash register sat on the counter. The room was empty, except for a few torn vinyl kitchen chairs and a cigarette ashtray stand that were positioned in front of the window facing the pump, no doubt a good place to watch for customers. Maps of Tennessee were placed neatly in a cardboard holder on the counter.

Empty shelves lined the wall to the left of the counter. Dub said that a long time ago the shelves used to be stocked with candy bars, chips, and little packaged cakes. When people would stop to gas up, he explained, they'd come inside to use the toilet or to stretch their legs and visit, and they would usually buy something to eat right then or to snack on later down the road. An empty glass refrigerator was next to the shelves.

"This room here was called a mart," Dub explained. "It was like a small grocery store, but not really. The story goes that Minner wanted to buy Clyde's grocery store but he wouldn't sell it, so Minner put food in his place to take away some of Clyde's business. It worked good, too. But James, he didn't do much with the mart."

Behind the window-enclosed mart was a bedroom with a full bed, dresser, and lamp. On the wall across from the bed was a short kitchen counter with a coffee pot, sink, and shelves for dishes. Next to it was a small refrigerator and large stove.

Annie and the kids were relieved to see the bed, but she shrieked with excitement when she saw the bathroom. It was small and smelled faintly of urine, but it had a sink and a toilet. Behind the door was a tub. She had never seen one before.

Annie and the boys didn't have any desire to investigate the huge garage that was attached to the mart. Dub told them that he had been using it to house his ambulance and wrecking truck for years. James never charged him for the space, either. He could hardly ring up the cash register with his coiled up hands, much less work on cars. So Dub agreed that it would benefit the residents of Cook by keeping his emergency vehicles right in town.

"But you know," he said to Annie and the boys, "I think it was that ol' guy's way of havin' me around day-to-day. He had somethang for me to do almost e'vr time I saw him."

That was just like Dub, Annie thought. Always doing things for other people. When she smiled at him, he blushed.

When Dub finished showing them around, he went to his truck and got the blankets. They were clean, but smelled of cigarette smoke. Annie and the kids didn't care. They were used to bad odors.

Before he left, Annie had only one question for Dub. "Who's Tinker?" she asked, referring to the station's namesake, Tinker's Tow & Garage.

"I don't rightly know, Annie," Dub replied. "It's been that name fer as long as I kin remember. But some of the townsfolk say that Minner liked to 'tinker' with cars. That's 'bout all we know about any tinker."

That made sense, she thought. Then Dub had to leave, saying he'd be back in the morning with breakfast.

Annie washed the boys' feet and cleaned up Becky's and Will's soiled pants. She nursed the baby while the boys snuggled in the bed next to her. It didn't take long for them to fall asleep. The steady rain that was hitting the tin roof was hypnotic to the youngsters. But it took Annie a while to doze off. Her mind was going a mile a minute.

Of all the curious things that had happened prior to her leaving the Bartons' home, Robert's lighter was the most peculiar, she thought. She found it hard to believe that someone like Verneice would take up with a filthy, illiterate man like Robert. Verneice had indoor plumbing and a huge sunken tub to bathe in. Annie racked her brain trying to remember if Robert had ever come home clean or cleaner than usual.

No, he's always been a stinkin' mess.

But Annie knew that somehow he and Verneice were involved with each other. "If not for sex, then what?" she asked herself. She thought about all the times Robert screamed at her to "stay away from that Verneice whore." And that Mama D felt the same way. *They hated her!* Annie thought. *Why?*

Then Annie thought of something that turned her insides upside down and almost made her puke. She tasted the acid vomit in her throat but fought it back as she gently pulled back the covers, climbed over her sleeping children and stumbled in the dark trying to find her light source. The kerosene lamp was sitting on the dresser and she struck a match to light its wick. The lamp's glow was strong in the small room, so strong that she was afraid the children would wake up from its light, but they didn't budge from their curled up positions. Annie looked around the room for her pillowcase filled with clothes, but couldn't see it. Then she remembered that she had left it in the bathroom.

That's good, she thought. *I'll just take the lamp in there and close the door so the kids don't know I'm up.*

She found the pillowcase on the floor behind the door where she had placed it earlier. And the something that made her stomach flip-flop, the something that almost made her puke, was lying next to it. The book, with all its wisdom and words and images, had shown her something a long time ago that didn't register in her brain until now.

Annie was anxious to see it again. She opened the book to its first page and there it was, just as she suspected – Verneice's kitchen table. The same tablecloth, the same daisy-decorated plates, the same basket of yellow napkins and the identical salt and pepper shaker set shaped like tomatoes. Annie took the kerosene lamp from the bathroom sink's counter and brought it down to the floor where she was sitting for a closer examination of the book's page. In the brighter light, she could make out something silver on the table between the tomato-shaped shakers, something that was either the butt of a stainless steel knife or the bottom portion of a Zippo lighter.

The vomit was coming up into her mouth now. She scooted on the floor over to the toilet, lifted its seat, and heaved. While on the floor, she opened the sink's cabinet door and found a clean washcloth. She stood up, ran the cool water over the rag and wiped her face. She looked into the mirror over the sink, stared into her eyes and began talking to herself, hoping that she could come to some conclusion about the book and its purpose in her life.

It's some kind of magical thing, that's for sure. I can read because of it. I can talk better because of it. It has given me power in a lot of ways, but why? And who is doin' this? Jesus? It's gotta be Jesus. I have prayed so hard for Him to help me. He's gotta be behind all of this.

"Thank you, Jesus," she said, staring up at Heaven that she knew was probably above the bathroom's ceiling somewhere. "Thank you, Lord."

Then she blew out the wick on the lamp and crawled back into bed with the kids. She must have gone right to sleep because the next morning came fast. Not once during the night could she remember waking up or even dreaming. Evidently, the kids didn't either.

Dub banged on the front door of the station and Annie got up. She had slept in her clothes, so she went right to the door to let him in. It was dark and gloomy outside. He was sopping wet in the rain. She turned the key and opened the door, keeping her distance from him so he wouldn't smell her mouth that was dry and tasted like vomit.

"Hey, girl, how you doin' this morning?" he asked sweetly, pushing the blue raincoat's hood off his head, but leaving on his wet baseball cap.

"Oh, we're fine, Dub," Annie answered, covering her mouth as she spoke. "What time of day is it, anyway?"

"It's about ten. Are y'all hungry?" he asked.

"Well, I know I am, but the kids are still sleeping."

Dub saw the boys standing in the bedroom doorway that led into the mart. Dwayne was holding Becky.

"No, they ain't!" he said, motioning his head in their direction.

Annie turned to see the boys. "Are y'all hungry? Dub here wants to know."

Will ran to Dub and he picked him up in his wet arms. When Dwayne handed Becky to Annie, she felt her wet diaper.

"I'll be right back, Dub. Becky's soppin' wet, kinda like that weather out there."

"Yeah, the rain is all everybody's talkin' about. Pig Dog's swollen, and if it overflows, we got some really big problems."

Annie couldn't remember the last time the creek overflowed, but she had heard stories from Daddy Jack and Mama D. It caused a lot of people to lose their crops and even killed a few children who were swept up by the raging water.

Dub went out to his truck and brought in two sacks of groceries. Annie saw them on the counter when she came out from the bedroom. She was holding Becky across her chest, but a towel covered the baby's head. Dub knew the child was getting her morning milk and he blushed at the thought of the baby sucking on Annie's nipple.

"What's this?" Annie said. "Groceries? Dub! How am I gonna pay you?"

"Yer not," said Dub. "It's a housewarming gift. Ev'r heard of that, Annie?"

She shook her head.

Dub unpacked the groceries onto the counter – milk, eggs, cereal, packaged donuts, bread, jelly, cheese, butter, coffee, sugar, and apples. "I called a buddy with the power company and asked him to switch on the electricity. It should be on now," he said.

He walked over to the switch near the front door and flipped it, illuminating the whole place like a circus ride. "Wow! Will ya looky here, Annie?" he asked. "That means the refrigerator is workin', too. Open it."

Annie walked back to the bedroom and opened the small refrigerator door. It was as cold as Verneice's house. "It's on!" she yelled to Dub in the other room.

"Thar's another one out here, Annie," he yelled back, "but it ain't plugged in."

The glass refrigerator in the mart lit up as soon as Dub put the plug in the wall. He put the groceries that needed to stay cool on the racks inside.

Becky finished nursing and Annie brought out a blanket from the bedroom for the baby to play on while she fixed breakfast for her and the boys. She found bowls and spoons in the cupboard and poured cereal and milk into two of them. There wasn't a table to sit at, so the boys sat on the floor and ate their cereal. Dub made coffee. Annie toasted bread and spread jelly on the slices.

Then the headlights of Sheriff Haynes' police car illuminated the mart when he drove his vehicle into the station's lot next to Dub's truck. He ran to the door in the pouring rain and walked in without knocking, dripping water onto the floor from the curled up sides of his cowboy hat. Dub, Annie, Dwayne, and Will stopped chewing their food because they were afraid he had come to tell them that they had to leave.

"Mis' Annie, Dub," the sheriff said, removing his hat. "Sorry to barge in like this, but I really need to talk to you, Dub. Is there somewheres we can go?"

"Sure, Larry," Dub replied. "How 'bout we go in the garage and talk?"

The men went into the adjacent garage where Dub's two emergency vehicles were parked. The rain was pounding louder there.

"Whut's up, Larry?" Dub asked.

"We got a body, Dub. Only it *ain't* a body. It's just bones. They warshed up outta Pig Dog this morning."

"How many bones you got?"

"The whole damned skeleton, Dub."

"You mean the whole skeleton done warshed up outta the creek at the same time? Ain't that kinda peculiar?"

"Yeah, it is," the sheriff replied. "It was the weirdest thang I ever saw. Thar it was, all in one piece, I tell ya, clingin' to this huge tree root at the top of the bank. The water had swept most of the tree's root away and left these big ol' stems stickin' out, and that skeleton was . . . well, damn it, Dub! That skeleton was hangin' on to it. I swear! That's the best I can explain it. The damn skeleton was hangin' on to the root vine!"

Dub had seen a lot of strange things in his days running a wrecker service and an ambulance, but a skeleton hanging onto a tree root took the prize.

"Folks'll be talkin' 'bout this one for a long time, eh, Larry? How'd y'all find it?"

"I got a call this mornin' from Lem Smithers' boy, Tim," the sheriff said. "His daddy sent him out with their two 'coon dogs to check the creek to see how high the water was and them two dogs spotted it across the creek. They were barkin' fools, those dogs."

"How'd y'all get it out?" Dub asked.

"Waal, I got Clyde up outta bed and we went over thar. Clyde's the one that come up with a plan to scoop it up. He took off to his store and got this big ol' butterfly net that someone ordered from the catalog but hadn't picked up yet. We stood on the edge of the creek bank and scooped the bones up in the net, and then laid 'em on the ground a'back from the creek. We covered it like we'd cover a body with flesh still on it."

"That's good," Dub said.

"But, Dub, let me tell you somethin' I ain't ever told no man alive," the sheriff said. "That skeleton spooked me. Ain't nothin' like I ever witnessed b'fore."

"Whadda'ya mean, Larry?"

"Okay, this here ain't for repeatin."

"Okay," Dub promised.

"Waal, that there skeleton was all in one piece, right? It was hangin' onto that root like a person, but git this. As soon as Clyde scooped it up and laid it on the ground, it fell apart. Jest fell the hell apart. Waddn't even connected no more. Jest a pile of bones. Now don't you think that's spooky, Dub? Like voodoo magic or somethin'?"

"That's weird shit, all right, Larry," agreed Dub. "Whar's it now?"

"I got men watchin' over it. We need your ambulance to take it to Herndon. Gotta be official, an all. And believe me, Dub, the sooner we get it the hell outta that field the better I'm ah'gonna feel."

"Okay," Dub said. "What part of Pig Dog are the bones laid out?"

"It's on the bank behind the Bartons' house."

28 / THE BODY

Mama D and Daddy Jack weren't even aware that townspeople were gathering in the field behind their house. The thunder was loud and the rain was pelting their roof hard, and their hearts ached too badly to care about anything but Robert.

They missed Annie's cooking and Daddy Jack was a poor replacement in the kitchen. He brought Mama D breakfast in bed but she wouldn't eat it.

"Ar' you tryin' to kill me?" she screamed when she saw the runny, greasy eggs and burned toast. "Jest brang me some cold cereal. Think ya kin do that? Jest brang me *anythang* but this here slop! Them hogs of yern wouldn't ev'n eat this shit!"

A loud clap of thunder shook the rickety house. Daddy Jack returned to the kitchen but needed a smoke first before he tackled round two of breakfast. Mama D hated his cigarettes and tolerated his smokes only when she was in a good mood, which wasn't often. So he decided to light one up on the back porch with the kitchen door shut, so she wouldn't raise a fuss.

While puffing his Lucky Strike and blowing the smoke outside through the screened door, he saw people with umbrellas walking down his gravel driveway toward the dirt path that ran alongside his house. Curious, he grabbed a coat from a nail on the porch and threw it over his head to shelter him from the hard rain.

He walked across the yard toward the driveway and saw Dub's ambulance parked at the end of it. He continued past the rows of vegetables, the barn and finally beyond the outhouse. He noticed that part of his chicken wire fence had been trampled down, no doubt by the trespassers who were huddled on the creek bank. About thirty people were standing around, some looking down at the ground and others pointing toward the creek. As he walked closer, he recognized Dub from his ball cap's brim sticking out from under his hooded raincoat. Then his eyes focused on the covered object on the ground and he got jittery.

"Hey, Dub!" he hollered. "Thatta body?"

Dub was reluctant to talk to Daddy Jack, but he decided to be professional, for his sake and for Annie's. After all, he *was* there on an official request from the sheriff and it *was* his job to transport the body to the medical examiner in Herndon.

"Hey, Jack," Dub replied. "Yeah, we got us a victim. Don't know who, though."

Daddy Jack was relieved that it wasn't Annie or one of her boys, but was puzzled about the condition of the body and why no one could recognize it.

"Don't know who?" he asked. "That bad, huh? Kin y'all tell if it's a man or a woman?"

"Naw," Dub answered.

"Waal, how 'bout I see if I knowed?" he asked.

"That ain't a good i-dee, Jack."

"Aw, c'mon," he pleaded.

Half the town had seen the skeleton already, Dub thought. It wasn't like they were exploiting the body and charging money to see it. Maybe Jack *could* recognize it somehow.

"Oh, all right, c'mon," Dub said.

Dub bent down and lifted up the orange tarp. Daddy Jack was surprised to see a mass of bones instead of a mangled body of half-decayed flesh that no one could identify. He walked over closer and knelt down next to it to get a better look.

Suddenly, he spotted something familiar and fell back, landing on his butt in the wet field. He looked up at the faces in the crowd who were looking down at him, hopeful that Jack knew who it was.

"Why, y'all know who this is, don't ya?" he asked.

"Naw," someone yelled out. The rest shook their heads 'no.'

"Only one person in Cook's got teeth like that," Daddy Jack said. "This heer is Maydell, Maydell Stokes, Verneice's maw."

The crowd gasped. Clyde Tubbs hollered out so he could be heard above the driving rain. "Maydell? Did you say Maydell, Jack? You know that f'shore?"

"Yeah, Clyde," he hollered back.

Daddy Jack picked himself up from the ground and crouched over the bones, pointing to the opened mouth of the skull. "See that gold tooth right 'cheer?" he asked, pointing to a top incisor. "Me and Mama D carried her to Herndon to git it."

"Aw, c'mon, Jack, lots of people have gold teeth," hollered someone from the crowd.

"No, not like this one," Daddy Jack answered, shaking his head. "Maydell didn't have money fer a whole gold tooth, so's her dentist, he jest put gold on the outside fer her to see. Look fer yersef. It's not gold on the inside."

Several of the bystanders took a peek at the inside of the skeleton's mouth. They all agreed that there was gold on the outside and that there didn't appear to be any gold on the inside of the tooth.

"Thar's lots of reasons for that, Jack," explained Sheriff Haynes. "For one, we don't know how long the body's been out here. That tooth being half gold and half whatever could be from decomposin'. And second, some animal could've chewed on it for all we know or it coulda been hit by a rock in the creek's water."

He stopped for a moment and said, "And I ain't heard that Mis' Maydell died. Last I heard she was alive and kickin' and living with Verneice. Don't y'all think we'd all know if Maydell had died?"

He looked around the crowd for their response. They all agreed, and Clyde said he had proof.

"Her mail's still comin' in to Cook, and her monthly government check is still bein' sent," said Clyde, who knew everybody's business in the small town from the mail pieces he sorted each day at the back of his store.

"Okay, y'all. I could be wrong," Daddy Jack said, "but, Dub, when y'all carry these bones to Herndon, tell 'em to have Maydell's dental man look at the teeth. His name's Shelton, Newt Shelton. Jest tell 'em, okay?"

"Okay, Jack," Dub answered with a doubtful smirk.

Dub picked up the tarp full of bones and carried it across the field to the ambulance. The rain had kept him from driving right up next to the body like he preferred. He was afraid it would get stuck in the field's mud or get a flat tire from running over the chicken wire fence that was now mangled with sharp pieces of wire that protruded like nails. So he had parked the vehicle on the road and walked to the site of the body. It wasn't like it was an emergency or anything. There was no hurry to get the body to the hospital.

"Newt Shelton," Daddy Jack hollered as Dub closed the ambulance's back doors. "He's on Decker Street. B'hind the hospital. He'll tell y'all. I *ain't* crazy. It's Maydell all right."

Dub just waved at him as he backed the ambulance away. Sheriff Haynes walked toward Verneice's house and Clyde joined him. Daddy Jack knew he had aroused their suspicion and he hurried to catch up with them.

"Y'all ar' goin' to see fer yersef, ain't ya?" Daddy Jack asked them. "She ain't thar, I kin tell ya that. Why, me and Mama D ain't seen Maydell in pert neer a year."

"Go on home now, Jack," the sheriff said. "Let the law handle it from here. Go on home and tend to yer wife. She needs you there, ya hear?"

Daddy Jack couldn't wait to tell Mama D anyway. She'd back him up about that tooth. *They'll find out it's Maydell for sure.*

He climbed the steps of the back porch and reached for the screen door's handle. *Poor Maydell!* he thought. *Wunder how she died and landed in that thar field?*

Mama D was standing on the back porch looking through the screen for Daddy Jack when she spotted him coming. As soon as he opened the door, she pounced on him.

"Jest whar in the hell 'ave you been?" she asked. "I been waitin' on my cereal fer thirty minutes!"

"I plum fergot 'bout yer damned cereal," he barked, hanging up the wet coat on its rusted nail and walking into the kitchen. "Listen, I seen Maydell's bones."

Mama D's mouth dropped. A panicked look came over her face. She grabbed the back of the kitchen chair to balance herself. Daddy Jack helped her walk through the kitchen to the living room couch.

"Waal, hell, Mama D, I didn't knowed you cared a thang a'tall 'bout that woman," he said, putting a pillow behind her head and then squatting in front of her on the floor.

Mama D could hardly talk. "Jack," she said softly, *too* softly for Daddy Jack's liking. It scared him when she talked that way. "Jack," she said again, "tell me how they found her."

Daddy Jack started from the beginning, telling her how he was out on the back porch when he saw people walking down the driveway toward the creek . . . how he saw the group of people in the field . . . how he asked to see the body . . . how he bent down and recognized the top tooth . . .

Mama D grabbed Daddy Jack's upper arm and squeezed it hard. She rose from the couch, breathing heavily. "Tell me, Jack Barton," she said loudly in his face, "tell me that it wuzn't you that told 'em it wuz Maydell. Tell me it ain't so."

"Oh, yeah, I did," he said proudly. "I recognized that tooth straight-away. Told 'em so, too, I did."

Mama D put her hand over her eyes and fell back on the couch crying. Daddy Jack was baffled by her emotion because she didn't even react that way when her own son died.

"Whut's a'come over you, Mama D? Why you cryin' over that woman?"

Mama D let up a bit, grabbed a soiled handkerchief from her robe's pocket and wiped her eyes. "Jack, thar ar' some thangs I kept from ya," she confessed. "Thar ar' some thangs that didn't need to be knowed."

"Waal, okay, I kept some thangs from you, too," confessed Jack.

"Not like this, Jack."

"Tell me, hon," he said. "Whut could be so bad?"

Mama D blew her nose. It had been a year since Maydell had died, a horrible year of mental pain, plotting, scheming, lying and yelling.

"I killed her, Jack," she blurted out. "I killed Maydell."

Daddy Jack fell over onto the flowered linoleum floor of the living room and stared up at her. He ran his hands through his dirty wet hair and put his head down.

"I gotta have a smoke," he said. "And I don't give a shit if you don't like it."

He got up and walked into the kitchen, pulled out a chair from around the table and sat down. He searched a pocket in his wet overalls for his cigarettes, hoping to find a dry one. He found two and laid the others out on the table to dry. Mama D shuffled into the room and sat down across the table from him as he lit one up.

He took a few puffs, looking at the floor and up in the air like he was contemplating what to say to her. Then he looked her straight in the eyes. "How in the hell'd you kill Maydell?"

Mama D put her head down and fidgeted with her wet handkerchief. She spoke slowly, her lips trembling. "Jack, 'member 'bout a year or so ago, back when it got so blasted hot an' the crick dried up?"

Daddy Jack nodded. They had lost a lot of crop money because of that drought.

"Waal," Mama D continued, "Robert wuz watchin' some picture show on the TV and I wuz takin' a nap. I think you carried Annie somewheres, Lord knows whar. The young-uns, too. It was jest me and Robert home."

Yeah, Daddy Jack remembered that day well. It was the day he took Annie to the woods in the truck and screwed her like a dog. He was getting excited thinking about it and a smile came up on this face, then Mama D slapped her hand down on the table to get his attention.

"Anyways, this here man ah'come to the door. Me and Robert ain't nev'r seen him b'fore. He wuz drivin' this black car and lookin' fer Verneice. We told him he had the wrong house an' told him whar she lived. He said he knew that, but she waddn't home."

Daddy Jack raised his right eyebrow, his curiosity piqued by the story of the stranger. He lit another cigarette, anxious to hear what this man had to do with Maydell's bones being in the creek.

Mama D took in a deep breath, exhaled and continued. She was beaten down. Daddy Jack could see that in her face, the most beaten down he'd seen her since the day she had heard Minner had died.

"Waal, me and Robert wanted to know whut he wanted, so we ast. Lord, we got us an earful. He wuz this lawman from Memphis, only he had on reg'lar clothes. He said that Verneice had ordered 'bout four hundred dollars in makeup but nev'r paid fer any of it. Jest kept the stuff an' sold it and kept the money. He wuz a'lookin' fer her to collect. Ar' ya followin' me, Jack?" she asked.

"Oh, yeah," he answered.

"Waal, we said we'd tell her he wuz a'lookin fer her, then he drove off. Me and Robert sar her come home 'bout an hour later and we high-tailed it to her place. We went inside her house and she fell out and had a cuss fight with us. She said we wuz plottin' a'gin her and she started throwin' thangs at us. She ran in the kitchen and pic't up ah iron that wuz sitting on ah board and slung it 'crost the room. It jest missed me. So I pic't it up and throwed it back, but Maydell, she come out to see whut wuz goin' on, and the iron . . . the iron, it . . ."

Mama D broke down sobbing. Daddy Jack reached across the table and grabbed her hand. "Whut 'bout the iron, hon?" he asked, stroking her hand. "Whut 'bout the iron?"

Mama D pulled loose from his touch, got up from the table and walked around the kitchen. She stopped at the sink and stared out the window with her back to him. She looked at the rain falling outside and her eyes squinted to see Verneice's porch. She swung around and looked at Jack.

"I didn't know it wuz gonna hit Maydell, Jack," she confessed. "I didn't know she'd git in the way. That iron hit her head and knock't her down flat. Verneice was screamin' and cryin' an' makeup wuz runnin' down her face. She looked like'a racoon. Then she said her mama wuz dead."

Daddy Jack couldn't believe that she and Robert had kept a secret like that from him for so long. He didn't know what hurt more, knowing that Robert was in on Maydell's death, too, or that his wife had caused the fatal blow.

"Then whut?" he asked.

"Waal, we stopped yellin' an' come up with an i-dee. Me and Robert give her four hundred dollars for the man in the dark car so she'd keep her mouth shut. Then when it fell dark, Robert and Verneice buried Maydell in the dried up crick bed."

"Ar' you shore that's all?" Daddy Jack asked. "You ain't holdin' back nothin' else?"

Mama D shook her head. "But it wuzn't the end, Jack. That bitch ast us fer money ev'r month. That's why we ain't had no money. She done took it all. Whut's gonna hap'n now, Jack? What ar' we'ah gonna do?"

Daddy Jack paused to think the situation through. He knew Verneice was not going to keep her mouth shut when the sheriff came knocking at her door and asking questions about her dead mother who she never reported missing. They were both doomed, and Robert would be, too, if he hadn't died.

"Ain't no way 'round it, Dorthea. "Yer goin' ta jail."

29 / THE DREAM

Sheriff Haynes stood near Robert's casket, his clasped hands holding his straw cowboy hat below his belt. His balding head was bowed in prayer as he listened to the words of Pastor Russell who stood before the cluster of mourners at the gravesite.

It was a beautiful sunny day, about 75 degrees, with a cool breeze that smelled like the flapping of fresh, laundered sheets that had been washed in good, store-bought detergent. The sky was light blue with high, cotton puff clouds. The past week of rain had cleansed the air in Cook, bringing life back into its dry land, turning straw grass into lush green lawns and sprouting colorful flowers that had almost choked from lack of water. The only evidence of the heavy rain was the muddy earth on the cemetery's property.

Mama D and Daddy Jack sat in front of the flowered coffin holding hands, every now and then wiping their wet eyes and re-adjusting themselves in the uncomfortable metal chairs. They were the only ones sobbing. Annie and the children did not attend the funeral service at the church nor the graveside send-off. Dub thought it was best for her to stay away from her volatile mother-in-law and let Mama D bury her son in peace.

When the graveside service was over, Pastor Russell closed his Bible and walked around the casket to Robert's parents to offer his condolences. He grabbed Mama D's hand and bent down to look into her eyes, saying soothing words about Heaven and Jesus and how Robert was in a better place. Everyone else walked away, except the sheriff. He waited until the preacher left before he approached the Bartons.

Mama D and Daddy Jack sat and stared at the casket for a few minutes before getting up to leave. Sheriff Haynes made his way over to them when they got up to walk to their truck. They stopped and turned in his direction. They knew what he wanted.

"Dorthea, Jack, I'm sorry for yer loss," he said sincerely.

Daddy Jack looked at him and nodded, extending his hand to the sheriff to shake. Then he put his arm around his wife's shoulder and they turned toward their truck.

"Uh . . . Dorthea," the sheriff said.

The couple stopped and turned. She looked at him, sobbing. "Uh . . . I'm sorry, Dorthea, but yer . . . yer . . . yer under arrest."

He reached in his right back pocket and took out handcuffs. "I gotta take you in."

The sheriff took Mama D's hands and placed them in cuffs behind her back. She didn't put up a fight. Neither she nor Daddy Jack said a word.

"Do you understand whut this is about, Dorthea?" the sheriff asked.

"Yeah," she said softly.

"Ah, c'mon, Larry," Daddy Jack said. "She ain't gonna run from ya. Take 'em cuffs off 'er, will ya?"

"Sorry, Jack, it's the law. I gotta carry her in my car, too. Yer welcome to follow us to Herndon. That's whar she'll be booked."

"But it wuz ah accident, Larry!" Daddy Jack pleaded.

"That's fer a court of law to decide."

Sheriff Haynes placed Mama D in the backseat of his police car and drove away. Daddy Jack followed close behind him. Dub watched the arrest unfold from his truck parked nearby. Earlier that morning the sheriff had asked him to stay behind after the funeral in case the Bartons got nasty. But now that they were safely on their way to Herndon, Dub could leave and give Annie the news. But first he was going to get Becky's crib at the Bartons' house.

Annie didn't have a clue about Maydell's death. She and the boys had spent the previous rainy day cleaning the old gas station and setting up house. They swept and mopped floors. They dusted. They cleaned the toilet and the bathtub, the refrigerator and sinks, and washed a pair of sheets that were on the bed. Annie made a clothesline out of rope and strung it across the mart. She washed their dirty clothes, towels and Becky's diapers and hung them on the line.

On the day of Robert's funeral, Annie awoke to the sun streaming in through the station's windows, sending rays of hope and renewal through her. She was giddy, happy to be alive, free of enslavement from the Bartons, and excited about what the future might hold for her and the children.

Dub pulled up about eleven o'clock. Annie and the kids were outside the station picking up trash that cluttered the front of the station around the gas pump. Becky squealed when she saw her crib in the back of his truck.

"Dub!" Annie yelled. "I can't believe it!"

Dub opened the door and stepped out. Will and Dwayne grabbed his legs and Annie threw her arms around his neck. Becky screeched from a blanket nearby where she was sitting.

"They let you have it? Mama D let you have the crib?" she asked excitedly, looking into his happy eyes.

"Waal, not really," Dub said, as he walked to the back of the truck to unload it. "It's a long story, Annie. I'll tell ya inside, okay?"

"Okay," agreed Annie. "I got a pot of coffee on the stove."

"Great. C'mon, boys, let's go get this thang set up," he said.

Annie picked Becky up from the blanket and all of them went into the station. The boys ran into the bedroom and jumped up in the bed. Annie placed Becky in the middle of the bed with them and told them to hold onto her while she moved some things around. She cleared away a small table next to the bed and the window, making a nice corner spot for the crib.

"Look here, Becky girl, you got a window, too!" she said to her baby.

Becky clapped her hands. The boys cheered.

It was lunchtime, so Annie fed the kids and Dub, and then put the children down for a nap. Dub went to the chair near the station's window and told her to join him. He saw the cigarette stand and decided that what he was about to tell Annie warranted a smoke. She sat down and smiled at him, grateful for all he had done, and anxious to hear his "long" story.

"So tell me," she said. "Tell me how come she let you have the bed."

Dub took a drag on his cigarette and flicked the ash in the large ashtray. "Waal, it ain't nothin' yer gonna believe right off from the start, so jest listen," he warned her. "Jest listen."

He stood up, put his cigarette in his mouth, and straightened both legs of his jeans that had wrinkled up over his boots. Then he sat back down, took another drag and starting talking.

"Do you 'member yesterday when the sheriff came to the station?"

"Yep," Annie replied.

"Waal, he needed me to help carry a body to Herndon."

Annie's hand cupped her opened mouth. She spoke through her fingers. "Oh, my God, who was it?"

"Okay, this here is the part yer not gonna believe," Dub said. "It was Verneice's mother."

Annie gasped. "Verneice's mother? Maydell?"

"Yup, Maydell. Only she'd been dead right neer a year. All they found wuz her bones. Pig Dog done flowed over in back of yore house and her skeleton was hangin' on a warshed out tree root. Kin you believe it?"

Annie shook her head in disbelief. "No wonder I ain't seen her. No wonder . . ."

Dub interrupted her. "And guess who killed her, Annie? Guess who killed her and buried her in the crick?"

Goose bumps ran up Annie's arms. She got up from the chair and walked around the front of the station, rubbing her hands up and down her arms to chase the bumps away. She turned to Dub. "I don't know, Dub. Who?"

"Mama D. She killed Maydell, and Robert and Verneice buried her body in Pig Dog. Verneice confessed to the whole thang and she and Mama D are in the Herndon jail."

Annie's stomach flip-flopped. It was doing a lot of that lately, she thought. She rubbed both temples with her palms. Dub got up and put an arm around her.

"You okay, baby girl?" he asked. "Set back down and I'll finish the story."

Annie sat, her face expressionless as Dub told her how Mama D had slung the iron across the room and hit Maydell, how she and Robert gave Verneice money to keep her quiet, and how Robert and Verneice had buried the body in the dried up creek.

"And it was Daddy Jack who give us the clue 'bout who the bones were," laughed Dub. "Didn't take Maydell's dental man no time to i-dee her body."

Annie grew weaker and limper with each word from Dub's mouth. She felt like her energy was being sucked right out of her. She didn't want to hear anymore and told Dub she needed to lie down with the boys and absorb everything that he had said. She didn't know what it all meant for her and her future, but she just needed to lie down before she fainted.

Dub kissed her on the forehead and left, saying he'd be back in a few hours to check on her. He told her he was going to Verneice's house to find a picture of her mother for the morgue and for a reporter from the *Herndon Chronicle* who was writing a story about the murder. Verneice had given the sheriff a key to her house, and he had asked Dub to take care of it for him. Verneice was cooperating in every way she could, hoping it would work in her favor when the murder came to trial.

Annie staggered to the bed and nudged the boys to move over near the wall so she would have room to lie down. She was lying on her back staring up at the ceiling, her right arm over her head, her left arm covering her mouth. She went over and over in her head everything that Dub had told her, finding it hard to believe and trying to make sense of the Bartons' actions over the last year.

No wonder Mama D hated Verneice!

She thought about all the mornings that she had risen early and bathed in the creek, probably right above Maydell's body. Maybe even Maydell's bones were floating around the water when she was bathing! She cringed at the thought of a skeletal hand coming up out of the water and grabbing her throat as she floated on her back.

Her brain zapped with an image of something white . . . a puffy cloud high above the creek's water, an object that flashed in her head every now and then, and one that she had believed was part of a dream.

She concentrated hard on the vision, recalling more images: a mushroom-like stalk coming out of the water . . . a flickering light at the bottom . . . her body frozen in its place on the creek bank as she watched a light trickle up a stalk that had emerged from the water, and how that light somehow transformed the marshmallow puffs of white at the top into a ball . . . and then seeing the ball transform to the figure of a woman, a woman whose piercing eyes were beautiful, yet familiar. They stared right into hers.

It all seemed so real, she thought. Not a dream at all. It was like she was actually there. But lots of her dreams were like real, she thought. Many of them were so real that when she awoke, she had a hard time shaking the images from her head.

But bits and pieces of this dream never seemed to go away. They kept coming back over and over a little at a time, and now she was able to pull some of the pieces together. She could recall more detail now and make out the woman's face clearly. She couldn't have made up such a beautiful vision on her own, she thought. Maybe it wasn't a dream after all. What she couldn't understand was why pieces of it floated around in her head for so long without coming together until now.

It was strange, she thought, that the book had come into her possession right after the image in the creek appeared. The day she saw the cloud was the day she found the book — she was sure of that now — the magic book that taught her to read, write and learn about the world. Could it all be a coincidence or could the lady in the cloud be connected in some way?

She got up from the bed and quietly searched for the book. Where had she put it? She remembered looking at it the night before in the bathroom when she had recognized a table setting on its first page that was identical to the one in Verneice's kitchen.

Annie searched through the entire gas station that she and the boys had cleaned earlier that day. She tore through cabinets and looked under the bed. The pillowcases that held their belongings when they fled the Bartons' house were empty and clean, folded in a drawer.

"Where is that dang book?" she said, frustrated.

While searching inside the mart's counter, she heard the garage door rise and thought it was probably Dub getting into one of his vehicles that were parked there. She opened the door leading from the mart to the garage and saw him approaching the driver's side of the ambulance.

"Hey!" she yelled.

"Hey, yourself," he said, turning around in her direction. "I thought you was layin' down."

"I was. But now I'm awake with lots of questions stirring in my head."

"Yeah, me, too."

"You headed to Herndon?" she asked, walking over to his vehicle.

"I gotta take these pictures over thar and then bring someone back." He held up a cigar box that Annie assumed contained pictures of Verneice's mother. "Y'all wanna ride along?" he asked.

"The kids are still sleeping."

When Dub opened the ambulance's door, the box fell from under his arm. Annie bent down to help him pick up the scattered photos.

"Geez, look at Verneice," she said, holding up a photo of a little girl maybe ten years old.

"That's her all right," said Dub, laughing. "Look at that damn purse she's holdin'."

They both laughed. The little girl was holding a flashy purse that was too big for her tiny body. It was covered with flowers and sequins.

"How come you got all these pictures?" Annie asked. "I thought the paper man only wanted her mama."

"No time to go through 'em all. They kin do that," he said.

The photos had scattered over the garage floor and even under Dub's ambulance. As they picked up each one, they had to blow dirt off before putting it back. When it looked like all of them were safely back in the box, Dub got in his ambulance and backed out of the garage.

"I'll see ya later, okay?"

"Okay," Annie said, waving good-bye.

"Oh, can you get the door? Just grab the rope and pull it straight down."

Annie reached for the rope and the door slid closed. As she was walking through the garage to the mart's door, she saw a small, white piece of paper on the floor where Dub's ambulance had been parked.

"We missed one," Annie said. "But he's got enough."

She picked up the photo that was lying face down on the dirty garage floor and turned it over and blew off the dirt. Annie looked at the woman's face and strained her eyes to see more clearly. She used the bottom of her blouse to swipe the picture clean.

She was stunned to see the familiar face.

"This can't be!" she said aloud. "I *am* seeing things now."

She walked over to the garage door to look at the photo in the sunlight that was streaming through the windows.

Yes, it was her, she was sure of that. She could never forget those kind eyes. She smiled at the photo and tears filled her eyes.

It was the old lady from the hospital waiting room who had helped her fill out the admittance form for Will, the sweet woman who made dots on the paper for her to trace. The woman she had tried to find later but couldn't to return her handkerchief, the sweet smelling handkerchief embroidered with daisies that she hid under her mattress at the Bartons' house so Mama D wouldn't find it.

Annie turned the photo over. Written on the back was the woman's name and a date: "Maydell, 1961."

Annie fainted, falling onto the garage's concrete floor.

30 / THE KNOT

As Dub's ambulance turned off the tarred road out of Cook onto the highway to Herndon, he reached for his sunglasses that were usually on the front seat next to him.

"Dagnabbit!" he said, beating the steering wheel with his hand. "I musta left 'em in the dang truck."

Dub made a U-turn in the middle of the highway and drove back toward Cook to get the glasses out of his truck, which he had parked at the gas station. He pulled up in front of Tinker's Tow and looked inside, but could see no one. He figured Annie and the kids were in the bedroom out of sight. He walked over to his truck and grabbed the glasses off the seat, then decided to see if the boys were awake and wanted to go for a ride.

No one came to the door when he knocked, so he walked in, hollering for Annie. He peeked into the bedroom and saw all three kids sleeping soundly. The bathroom door was open. But no Annie.

There was only one other place she could be, he thought: the garage, where he had left her twenty minutes earlier. As he opened the mart's door that led to the garage, he saw Annie's feet on the ground behind his tow truck.

Dub rushed over to her and saw a small puddle of blood on the cement floor near her head. He couldn't tell if she had fallen or if someone had hit her. He picked up her wrist to feel a pulse and it was faint.

"Yer alive, baby girl," he said relieved. "Yer alive. Thank you, God."

Dub, now in high gear with a dose of adrenalin flowing through every vein, knew he had to get Annie to the hospital. He pulled up the garage door, ran to the ambulance, and opened its back doors. Then he ran back for Annie and carried her to a cot inside the emergency vehicle.

He didn't have time to wake up the children and drag them along, but he couldn't leave them alone, either, so he drove to the preacher's house to get help. He left the ambulance's motor running while he ran to the front door, frantically beating on it and yelling for help. Pastor Russell's wife, Vera, answered and she said she and her husband would be happy to go to the station and get the children. Dub jumped back into the ambulance, turned on its loud siren and headed to Herndon General Hospital.

He had taken that route a thousand times or more but never with such a precious cargo. He loved her, he was sure of it. He had never felt so close to anyone in his life. He thought about her all the time, recalling special moments, laughter, and conversations over and over in his mind. Whether he was asleep or awake, Annie was always with him.

Dub wasn't sure if Annie felt the same way about him, but he knew there were *some* feelings. He thought about how her eyes lit up when he brought over the crib and how she had thrown her arms around him. How he had kissed her forehead and tasted her sweat on his lips, and the way she looked at him from time to time. He wanted to marry her, to take care of her and the kids, to spend the rest of his life sleeping next to her in the same bed. Maybe even have more kids. He would be a good husband, no doubt about that, and he'd love her in a way that Robert never did.

"Oh, Annie girl," he said aloud. "I love you so much."

Annie stirred in the cot and moaned, as if she had heard her name mentioned. He was glad to hear her moving about, and his foot pressed down harder on the accelerator.

The hospital's staff had heard the siren blaring and greeted Dub's ambulance at the emergency doors. They rushed the gurney inside to a prepared room and shooed Dub away.

"We'll take it from here, Dub," the nurse said. "Are there any kin on their way to fill out her admittance form?

"Naw," Dub said. "She's a friend o' mine and I brung her in alone."

"Well, I gotta have some information on her, Dub. Go out yonder and fill out the paperwork so we know who she is and who her next of kin is.

Can you do that?"

"Yeah," answered Dub.

"Oh, and one more thing," the nurse added. "We've got a patient ready to ride back with you. You'll see him in the waiting room."

Dub didn't want to leave Annie, but he thought that by the time he got back from taking his rider to Cook she would be fixed up like new and ready to go home. So he left her there in what he knew were good hands.

As the nurses cleaned Annie's head wound, they kept poking her and asking questions that required her to respond. All she wanted to do was sleep. About thirty minutes later, she felt a hand gently pressing her upper arm and shaking her to wake up. She smiled as she inhaled the familiar scent of Dr. Shea's cologne.

"Hello, again," Dr. Shea said when Annie's eyes opened and stared into his. "We've got to stop meeting like this."

Annie managed a faint smile. "Dr. Shea," she said softly. "I thought you were going to California."

"Almost," the doctor said. "I had to postpone my departure until the hospital found a replacement. And I'm glad I did because now I can properly tell you good-bye."

For a moment, Annie thought she might be dreaming. "Is this a dream?" she asked.

"I'm afraid not. You have a mild concussion from a fall. The ambulance driver, I think Dub is his name, found you on the floor of a gas station. Do you remember falling?"

Annie thought a minute. Her head was clouded with pain and the light over her bed was burning her eyes. She remembered the photograph with Maydell's name on it.

"Yeah, I remember," she said, lightly touching the bump protruding from her right temple. "A lot of things have happened to me lately and I guess I'm just plumb tuckered out."

Dr. Shea laughed at her choice of words. "You're tuckered out, all right! That's a pretty 'plumb' concussion you've got, too. I'm afraid I can't let you leave until we observe you overnight."

Annie grabbed her head and gasped. "Oh, my God! The kids! Who's got my kids?"

Dr. Shea sat down on the side of her bed, grabbed her arm at the elbow and pulled it away from her head. "I'm not sure, Annie, but . . ."

Just then the curtain around her bed opened in the middle. Dr. Shea turned to see Dub standing there smiling, holding Becky in his arms. Will and Dwayne stood at his side. The boys ran to their mother.

"Did you git a sucker, Mama?" Dwayne asked.

Dr. Shea stood up and reached into his pocket for a sucker for each of the boys, then pulled Will up into his arms. Dub walked over and handed Becky to her mama.

"I'll let you enjoy your family now," said Dr. Shea, placing Will on the bed with the other two children.

"You take good care of your mama, you hear?" he said to Will.

"Yessir," he replied.

He reached across Annie's bed to shake hands with Dub. "It's Dub, right?" he asked.

"Yessir."

"I've seen you come and go for the last year, but can't say that I've ever had the pleasure."

"Me neither," said Dub, shaking his hand.

"We'd like to keep Annie overnight. She's got a concussion, a little worse than Will here had, but it's nothing to treat lightly."

"Okay. I thought that might happen, so I got some folks to take the young-uns."

All three of the children clung to Annie in the bed, stroking her arms and face with their tiny hands. Annie brushed Becky's hair with her fingers and caressed Dwayne's back. Dr. Shea looked at them for a moment and sighed.

"I hope my fiancée and I have children who are so loving," Dr. Shea said.

Then he walked through the open curtain and out the door. Annie stared at the white ceiling like she was in a trance.

"How you doin', hon?" Dub asked.

She had a headache, but that was all. "Fine," she answered, still staring upward. "Just fine now that I got the kids."

Then her eyes moved to connect with Dub's. "Thanks for bringing them, Dub."

"Aw, it wuzzn't nothin'," he said, blushing.

"Say, Dub, can I ask you somethin'?" she asked.

"Sure."

"What's a fiancée?"

Dub took off his ball cap and scratched his head. "I'm not fer shore, but I think it's someone yer gonna marry, and yer a *fee-on-see* until you tie the knot. And I think it's a French word."

Engaged? Annie had no idea that Dr. Shea was *engaged!* He never mentioned a woman in his life, but then why would he? She was just a patient of his. But he did go out of his way to help her with the legal papers. And he did come all the way out to Cook to check on Will. And he did kiss her on the forehead.

What was I thinking? she thought. *What the hell was I thinking, that the handsome doctor wanted to marry me or something? Take me and the young-uns out to California? Be a doctor's wife? Wear fancy clothes and drive a pretty car? Live in a big house?*

"Whut'cha thinkin' 'bout, Annie girl?" Dub asked, interrupting her thoughts.

"How lucky I am to have y'all. That's all."

He bent down and kissed her forehead. *I know I heard right*, Dub thought, as he pressed his lips on the woundless side of her head. *I know I heard her say y'all.*

That means me, too. Y'all means me, too.

31 / THE SURPRISE

The first thing that Annie saw when she woke up the next morning in the hospital was a colorful bouquet of flowers on a table across the room. She pulled herself up in the bed to get a better look at them because her vision was a little fuzzy and the room was dark because the curtains were closed. But her head throbbed, so she slowly lowered herself back down. She stared up at the ceiling and fought back tears. She worried about her children who had spent the night with strangers.

A nurse knocked lightly on the door and then entered. "Well, I see you're awake!" the nurse said, walking to the window and pulling back the drapes to allow the morning sun to shine in the room. "I bet you're real hungry, too, huh?" she asked, removing a metal clipboard that was hanging at the end of Annie's bed.

Annie covered her eyes with her hands when the sunlight hit her face. "Yes," she replied, faintly. "I'm a little hungry."

After scribbling a few things on the paper that was clipped to the board, the nurse walked over to Annie's right side. She reached into the oversized pocket on her smock and took out a glass stick and placed it in Annie's mouth. Annie sucked on it.

"No, no!" the nurse said laughing. "Don't suck on it!"

She pulled the thermometer out. "I'm going to put it back in, but this time hold it under your tongue, okay?" she instructed.

"Okay," Annie replied. "I'm sorry."

"No reason to be sorry," she said. "I guess I should have explained, but it's just that I don't treat too many patients these days who haven't had their temperature taken."

As Annie held the thermometer in place, the nurse took ahold of

Annie's wrist with her right hand and stared at her watch on her left arm.

"Looks good," she said, placing Annie's arm on the bed when she finished. She removed the thermometer and wrote on the clipboard again.

"The doctor is going to come by in a few minutes and release you from the hospital. In the meantime, though, you've got a visitor outside who needs you badly."

When the nurse opened the door to leave, Dub was standing there with Becky in his arms. The baby squealed when she caught sight of her mother.

"Hey, baby girl," Annie said smiling. "I bet you're real hungry, huh?" She reached out for the baby and Dub handed her over.

"Good thang you fed her last night 'cuz she ain't had nothin' since," said Dub. "She stayed with the preacher's wife last night and wouldn't suck a bottle to save her life."

Becky was pawing at her mother's hospital gown looking for her breakfast. Annie pulled it up and exposed her breast to Becky. Dub caught a glimpse and turned away. The hungry baby dove in.

"How are the boys, Dub?" she asked, above Becky's slurping sounds.

"They're jest fine," answered Dub. "They had 'em a big ol' time over at Clyde's. You like the flowers?"

"They're beautiful, Dub. Did you bring them?"

"Yup. Got 'em at a flower store here in Herndon," he said. "I thought you might notta had any flowers like this heer in yer life."

"Never, Dub. No one's *ever* given me flowers."

"I brung you something else, too," he said excitedly, holding up a grocery sack he had carried in with him. "The preacher's wife sent you a purdy dress to wear home. She guessed at yer size and says she hopes it fits. She even sent some shoes."

Annie stared at Dub with a puckered face that was about to explode in tears. "I don't even know that woman, Dub," she said with a slight hoarseness. "And she's given me clothes to wear?"

"Yeah, Annie girl, and that's not all," he added. "We got a big surprise fer ya at home."

Annie cleared her throat and her voice was more energetic. "Tell me, Dub. C'mon, tell me, what kind of surprise?" she pleaded.

"Now, if I tell you it won't be a surprise, Annie! As soon as Becky's done eatin', we can take you home and you'll see whut . . . "

Dub stopped talking when he heard three soft knocks on the door.

"Come on in," Annie said, thinking it was the nurse again.

"Good morning," said Dr. Shea, reaching for the clipboard at the end of Annie's bed so he could read the nurse's notes.

"Good morning, doctor," said Dub.

Annie looked down toward her baby to make sure her breast was not exposed. Becky was sucking loudly and both Dub and the doctor looked a little embarrassed by the sound.

"How are you feeling, Annie?" the doctor asked.

"I think pretty good, Dr. Shea. My head still hurts a little."

"Well, let's take a look," he said, walking toward her. He put his hand on her forehead and pulled the skin back above her eye with his thumb. Then he took a light from his pocket and shined it right into her eyeball. He repeated the same procedure on the other eye. Then he did a series of little tests with the light, telling her to look straight ahead, and then side to side, with her eyes following every move of the light.

He examined the knot on her temple and told her he had to listen to her heart and lungs. "As soon as the little one is finished with breakfast, that is," he said, laughing.

Annie pulled Becky off her breast, and the sound of her mouth being yanked from her nipple was like a moonshine bottle being uncorked. The unhappy baby came up from underneath her mother's gown with a wrinkled face and breast milk all over her mouth. She fussed because she wasn't finished nursing, so Annie handed her to Dub to take out into the hall.

Annie sat up in the bed. Dr. Shea put the cold stethoscope on her chest, asking her to breathe in deeply and then to exhale slowly with each placement of the round silver piece on her skin.

When he finished, he wrote down more information on the clipboard, returned it to the end of the bed, and then walked over to her right side and sat down. She brushed back her hair with her fingers and re-adjusted her gown and bedding. She was nervous with his body so close to hers.

This is good-bye, she thought, fidgeting with her sheet.

He reached over and pulled her chin up in his direction. She stared into his handsome face and felt limp, like all her muscles and bones had turned to jelly. His eyes were sad, she thought, and his top lip quivered a little. When he took in a large breath and exhaled through his nose, she could smell his morning coffee.

"Annie, I've never met anyone like you in my life," he said, still holding her chin in his hand. "You are strong and courageous, and a wonderful mother to your children."

Her eyes filled with tears and he let go of her chin so she could get a tissue from a box on the other side of her bed. She couldn't look at him, so she put her head down and wiped each eye. He stared out the window until she collected herself, then he turned his face in her direction.

"I have grown very fond of you, Annie," he said clearing his throat. "From the moment we first met, I felt this urge inside of me to protect you and keep you safe. I used to lie awake at night thinking about you in that house with your in-laws and how horrible that existence must be for someone like you."

Annie dabbed her eyes and raised her head. She put her head back on the pillow and looked into his eyes while he talked.

"I am going to California at the end of the week to start my practice, and in the fall I'm getting married. She's a good woman, Annie, but there are so many things about you that I wish she had. She's strong like you, but in a different way. She's a medical doctor, too, and I know that means she won't have dinner on the table every night at the same time or wash and iron our clothes or breast feed our children, because she won't be home to do all those things. And that's okay, you know? Because during the day we will be helping sick people."

Annie's tears had stopped and she smiled as he talked. She loved the sound of his voice and all his perfect words that flowed out of his mouth.

"You are the most selfless person I have ever met, Annie, and it's a quality that not everyone has. What amazed me in the beginning was that even though your husband and his parents were mean to you, you didn't take their meanness out on anyone. You were still a kind and thoughtful person. I was drawn to you because of that quality. I loved watching you with your children and seeing their love for you returned. And I know that any man who marries you will be the happiest man alive."

He stopped for a moment and gazed out the window again. She stared at his handsome profile and smiled at the way his hair formed a tiny curl behind his ear.

"I want you to know that meeting you has changed me in some way. It has made me a better person . . . not just for myself, but for my patients, too."

He bent down, kissed her forehead and looked into her eyes. "Thank you, Annie," he said. "Thank you for making me a better person."

Annie smiled and touched his arm. His skin was warm, and her body tingled as she touched his arm hair.

"You're welcome," she said affectionately, stroking his arm. "Thank you for caring about me and my children."

When their eyes made contact for a few seconds, she marveled again at the length of his eyelashes. Their gaze was interrupted when Dub rapped on the door and entered with a crying baby.

"She wants her mama!" Dub said, walking over to hand the squealing child to Annie.

As soon as Becky was in her mother's arms she quieted.

"So, Doc, can I take her home?" Dub asked.

"Dr. Shea looked at Annie. "You ready to go?" he asked.

"Yes."

"Then I officially release you to the world," he said laughing.

Dub shook the doctor's hand. "Thanks, Doc," he said.

"My pleasure."

Annie watched Dr. Shea walk out, knowing it was the last time she'd ever see him.

All the way back to Cook, Annie pestered Dub to tell her about the surprise, but he didn't budge an inch. She thought of all kinds of things it could be, but he just shook his head with each guess. "Even if you guessed it I wouldn't tell ya," he laughed.

They drove into the small parking area in front of the gas station and Will and Dwayne were sitting in front of the window waiting. They ran outside to greet their mother. Clyde's wife, Dora, was right behind them.

"Annie looked at Dora and smiled. "Thank you for watching my boys," she said.

"They are darlin' young-uns," Dora said. "They stayed with me and Clyde last night, and Becky, she stayed with my sister. Y'all go on inside now. The surprise is a'waitin'."

"C'mon, Mama," Dwayne said, pulling on her flowered sundress. "Wait 'til you see!"

Annie's stomach felt queasy. It always did that when she was nervous or anxious about something. She put her hand on her abdomen and took a deep breath. Before Dub opened the front door, he told her to close her eyes. "And don't open 'em 'till I tell you, okay?"

"Okay."

He guided her through the door, and as she entered, the delicious aroma of food filled her nostrils. She stepped slowly inside and Dub told her to open her eyes. When she did, she saw the happy faces of several townspeople standing around in the mart. They all yelled, "Surprise!"

Their loud voices startled Becky and she grabbed Annie tightly around the neck. Annie looked around the room and recognized only a few faces, but they all looked like nice people, smiling and clapping.

Clyde came out of the crowd and spoke in front of everyone. "Mis' Annie, we all got together last night and thought 'bout yer predickament an' all, yer husband dying, yer mother-in-law kickin' y'all out and then her gettin' arrested, then yer' fallin' and goin' to the hospital . . . anyways, we all wanted to do something for you. So we thought, 'How can we git this gal on her feet? Whut can she do to make money?' And you know whut?"

"What?" Annie replied.

"You make a mighty mean pecan pie."

The crowd burst out laughing. "And don't ferget the squirrel stew!" yelled someone from the crowd.

"Yeah," Clyde said. "And a great squirrel stew, too. So we thought ya might wanna make this here place into a diner."

Clyde motioned for the crowd to clear the way so Annie could see the rest of the mart. Card tables and chairs filled the empty space occupied yesterday by just two chairs and an ashtray stand.

A bewildered Annie could hardly talk. "Where did all this come from?"

"We brought them from our homes," Pastor Russell said. "And that one there came from Clyde's store." He pointed to the table that all the townspeople knew was a favorite one that had been used for years for dominoes and checkers on the grocery store's front porch. Now it was covered with a checkered tablecloth and decorated with placemats and dishes.

Dub stepped forward and hugged Annie who still held Becky in her arms. "Annie girl, Tim Smithers checked out yer stove and it runs good now. And Clyde here, he stocked yer shelves with all the stuff you need to cook with."

"And I brought'cha my granbaby's old high chair and playpen," Dora said.

"And I give ya our old TV," said a man Annie didn't recognize.

As they walked through the crowded mart to the bedroom area in the back, Annie admired all the beautifully set tables. Right outside the bedroom door was a pen filled with toys, and Becky pushed against Annie's body to get down into it and play.

"Go ahead, put 'er down," said Dora. "That's whut it's fer."

Annie put Becky in the pen and walked into the bedroom. A TV was set up near the bathroom door, the only spot left in the small room for any more furniture. The crowd stood behind her to catch a glimpse of her surprised face.

"Now, this here wall can be moved and a whole nuther room can be built on," said another man she didn't know, who made his way through the crowd and into the small room. "I can do that fer ya, no sweat."

"Now let's all go into the mart . . . I mean diner, and eat us some vittles!" yelled Dub, who Annie had somehow lost in the crowd.

Dora grabbed Annie's arm and led her to a special table they had set for her. "We cooked dinner fer you tonight, Annie. Jest set yerself down and let us git the grub, okay?"

"Okay," said Annie, feeling a little funny about not dishing up the food for everyone.

They all sat down except a few women who dished up the plates from the counter. Dub sat across from Annie. The boys sat on each side of her, and Becky sat in a highchair to her left playing with a small plastic dog.

"Dub, this was your idea, wasn't it?" she asked.

"Nope," he replied. "It shore wazzn't."

"Then who?"

"The preacher's wife, Vera, and Clyde's wife, Dora. They're sisters and they help lotsa people in Cook. Why, hell, Annie! You been holed up in that Barton house fer so long that you don't even know how great the folks here is. Why, Tennessee's got the best folks in the whole United States!"

"Heer, heer!" said a man at the next table, raising his glass of iced tea.

Annie had never experienced kindness of any kind from strangers. There was food enough to feed the whole town — fried chicken, meat loaf, gravy, mashed potatoes, white beans, corn on the cob, collard greens, turnips, pickles, cornbread, biscuits, and iced tea. Everyone ate so much it was a wonder anyone had room left in their stomachs for dessert — apple pie, homemade ice cream, and pralines.

"You can make a go of it, Annie girl," said Dub, as he smeared butter on his cornbread. "People will pay fer yer cookin', you'll see."

Annie wept into her napkin and her head throbbed with pain. Dora came over to see if she was okay, then motioned to several in the room to hurry up so Annie could lie down and get some rest.

Before they all left, the ladies covered the leftovers and set them in the mart's glass refrigerator. Dub helped Annie put the kids down for a late afternoon nap, and then they both sat down at one of the tables and talked. Annie had been dying to ask Dub about the newspaper article about Maydell's murder, but she was so overcome with emotion and gratitude that she had forgotten about it until now.

"Yeah, it come out in t'day's paper," Dub said when she asked about the reporter's article. "It's in my truck. Be right back." He got up and went outside.

Annie looked around the room at all the pretty tables. She kept pinching her arm to wake herself up, for she was sure this was all part of a dream.

"Here it is," said Dub, setting the paper on the table. "Right'cheer on the front page."

The article's headline read: "Cook Woman's Skeletal Remains Found in Creek." There was a picture of Maydell that she recognized from the one that had fallen out of the box onto the garage's floor, and unflattering photos of Verneice and Mama D. Inside the newspaper, where the story continued from the front page, was another photo, a snapshot of Maydell when she was a young schoolteacher in Cook. Beside her was a little girl that Annie recognized as Verneice.

It was just as Annie had suspected. She had a hunch that the young Maydell, the smart beautiful woman who taught all of Cook's children to read and write before and after the war, was the same woman she had seen in the creek atop the lighted stalk and marshmallow clouds. Maydell's eyes were the same as those that had stared into Annie's when she stood frozen on the creek bank.

Annie rested her elbow on the table and cupped her chin with her hand. She closed her eyes, smiled, and exhaled a tranquil sigh. She felt peaceful inside her body now. *It wasn't a dream, I'm sure of it now. The stalk, the cloud, the book, the old lady in the waiting room, the bones — it was real. And I owe it all to Maydell. No wonder I haven't seen the book since her bones were found! She doesn't think I need it anymore!*

There was just one thing left for Annie to do to prove her assumptions were right, she thought. She looked over at Dub who was smoking a cigarette and gazing out the window.

"Dub, will you do me a favor?"

"Anythang you want, sugar," he replied, blowing a smoke ring in the air.

"Will you go to Daddy Jack's and get something for me?"

"Sure. Whut?"

"See if Daddy Jack will let you go into my bedroom. Tell him it's real important. Once you get in there, go to the side of my bed that's near the window and reach under my mattress up by my pillow. Bring me what you find, okay?"

"Okay," he said, anxious to see what she was talking about.

Her mattress's treasure was the only tangible proof Annie had that the encounter with Maydell's spirit wasn't a dream.

Ten minutes later Dub was back. "This it?" he asked with a puzzled look, dangling the object from his fingers.

"Yes," she said, grabbing it from his hand. She cupped the white handkerchief in her left hand and peeled back each folded side until she saw the embroidered daisies.

Annie put the handkerchief to her lips and smelled its sweet scent, a smell so close to Dr. Shea's cologne it could have been the same. But she knew that it wasn't. That was impossible. She began to weep.

"Thank you, Maydell," she whispered into the handkerchief. "Thank you for my life."

A truck backfired out on the road and startled her. She looked out the huge picture window of Tinker's Tow with teary eyes and a throbbing head and saw a red car passing by. Dub saw it, too. "That's a pretty car," said Annie. "I've seen it before, I think. Do you know who owns it?"

Dub took off his ball cap and scratched his head. He knew who owned it. He'd seen Dr. Shea behind the wheel of that red Ford Fairlane many times around Cook.

"I don't rightly know, Annie," Dub said, shaking his head and avoiding her eyes. "I don't rightly know."

THE END